Fables from India

THE
HAPPY MONK

AND
OTHER STORIES

Other Titles in the *Fables from India* Series

A Crocodile Makes History and Other Stories
The Beginning of the Mahabharata and Other Stories
The Pillar of Justice and Other Stories

Fables from India

THE HAPPY MONK

AND
OTHER STORIES

BASED ON
INDIAN AFTER DINNER STORIES BY
A.S. PANCHAPAKESA AYYAR

COMPILED AND EDITED BY
TERRY O'BRIEN

RUPA

Published by
Rupa Publications India Pvt. Ltd 2013
7/16, Ansari Road, Daryaganj
New Delhi 110002

Sales centres:
Allahabad Bengaluru Chennai
Hyderabad Jaipur Kathmandu
Kolkata Mumbai

Edition copyright © Rupa Publications India Pvt. Ltd 2013

Selection and Introduction copyright © Terry O'Brien 2013

All rights reserved.
No part of this publication may be reproduced, transmitted, or stored in a retrieval system, in any form or by any means, electronic, mechanical, photocopying, recording or otherwise, without the prior permission of the publisher.

ISBN: 978-81-291-2073-1

10 9 8 7 6 5 4 3 2 1

Typeset by Innovative Processors, New Delhi

Printed at HT Media Ltd., Noida

This book is sold subject to the condition that it shall not, by way of trade or otherwise, be lent, resold, hired out, or otherwise circulated, without the publisher's prior consent, in any form of binding or cover other than that in which it is published.

Contents

Introduction vii

Escaped! 1
Why Not Sacrifice Your Father? 3
The Half Pomegranate 5
The Young Mother 6
Face Saving 8
Critics Silenced 10
War Prevented 12
A Robber Reforms 14
Caste at Source 17
Beauty Analysed 21
Gold is Cheap, Great Men Scarce 23
The Greatest Teacher Ever 26
The Evil One Conquers At last 27
Finding a New Spring 32
The Golden Plate 35
The Mouse Merchant 38
The Price Maker 42
Little Prince No-father 45
The One-hundredth Prince 48
The King With One Grey Hair 52
The Happy Monk 55
Beauty and Grey 59

Mountain Buck and Village Doe	62
The Wind-deer and the Honey-grass	65
The Fawn Who Played Hookey	68
The Fawn Who Played Dead	70
The Wind and the Moon	73
The Goat Who Saved the Priest	75
The God in the Banyan Tree	78
The Monkey King and the Water Demon	80
The Tree That Acted Like a Hunter	83
The Dog King Silver	85
The Great Horse Knowing-one	91
Dirty Bathwater	96
Ladyface	98
Best Friends	101
The Bull Called Delightful	104
Grandma's Blackie	107
Big Red, Little Red and No-squeal	110
Harsha's Experiments	112
Devotion Tells	114
Wings Not Grown Yet	116
Asoka and his Viceroys	117
The Perfect Wife	119

Introduction

India is a land of myriad colours. With its rich history of folklore, India abounds in stories that have enthralled readers from time immemorial.

The oral tradition of narrating stories has ensured that these stories have been passed down from generation to generation. This exciting collection brings together a few of these classic tales for the young reader.

Escaped!

When Siddhartha had become a sanyasi and was sitting one day on the Pandava rock near Rajagriha, King Bimbisara of Magadha was struck with his majestic and handsome figure and offered him his daughter and half his kingdom. Siddhartha replied, 'I am a prince and could have ruled a kingdom myself had I wanted to. I left it, oh king, in order to ponder on suffering and to find a remedy for birth, disease, old age and death.' 'But my daughter is charming,' said Bimbisara. 'She can't be more charming than Yasodhara, the mother of Rahula,' said Siddhartha. 'I have left her and him, abandoned father, wife, son and kingdom in the quest. So, King, I must decline your offer.' 'But, how can you wear these rough clothes; how can you eat the hotch-potch got from different houses by begging?' asked Bimbisara. 'At first, I felt these irksome. Now I am accustomed to them. The plain robes of a *Bhikshu* make me realise that clothes don't make a man, and that it is not what we eat but what we think that matters more. Honey is sweet, but it is the proceeds of robbery with murder. River water is sweeter because there is no robbery or murder,' said Siddhartha. 'Oh, when you discover the truth, you must tell me' said Bimbisara. 'It may take some years,' answered Siddhartha. 'I don't mind,' said Bimbisara. 'As a matter of fact, I have still a great fascination for strange women, and this may last for some years. If I accept your truth, I suppose I shall have to give up these forbidden pleasures.' Then he left.

Siddhartha began his terrible penance by the Neranjana river in the Uravela forest. He soon became a skeleton. News of this reached Suddhodana. He sent word to his son not to torture himself by penances and not to disgrace his clan and family by begging, but to return to the palace and his father, wife, son and kingdom at once. He sent a deputation of Sakya princes to wait on him and persuade him to go back. Siddhartha said to them. 'Tell my royal father that no prisoner who has escaped returns to his prison. I have escaped from the palace where lust burns as white heat, where the black cobra lives, where birth, disease, old age and death are ignored till they catch hold of their poor victims unawares. Will one who has escaped from a burning house return except to rescue his near and dear ones when he has gathered the materials with which to save them? I, too, shall find out a way to conquer suffering and then come back to Kapilavastu and rescue my dear father, beloved wife and darling child and you, my Sakya brethren.' 'But, Siddhartha, you may never discover the way. You may simply die by the side of this forest stream,' said the Sakyas. 'It does not matter,' replied Siddhartha. 'I shall not swerve from the path even if all my blood dries up and my flesh withers away and I die. That itself is escape from the prevailing lust, apathy and indifference. It is better to die in the field of battle than to live a defeated life.'

Why Not Sacrifice Your Father?

Bimbisara was about to sacrifice fifty goats. His palace priest was ready for the ceremony. At that moment, Buddha entered the sacrificial room and asked Bimbisara to stay his hand, since God, who created the goats, would ceretainly not be pleased if they were sacrificed. Bimbisara asked Buddha to argue the point with the high priest, and promised to abide by the opinion of the victor in the discussion. Buddha then asked the high priest 'Why, O high priest, do you sacrifice these poor animals?'

'Fool!' returned the priest. 'Three people profit by this sacrifice, and none lose by it. King Bimbisara earns merit, because he is the cause of this sacrifice. I gain merit, because I perform the sacrifice with my hands; and the goat, even the goat, benefits, since it enters Heaven by being sacrificed. Thus three gain, and none lose.'

'Do all those who are sacrificed gain Heaven?' asked Buddha. 'Assuredly, yes,' replied the priest. 'There is not the least doubt about it.'

'Is your father living?' asked Buddha. 'Yes,' replied the priest. 'You want him to enter Heaven, don't you?' asked Buddha. 'Of course, I do,' replied the other.

'You know that, in the ordinary course of things, you cannot be certain about his going to Heaven,' said Buddha.

'True,' said the high priest.

'Then, why not sacrifice your father and ensure him Heaven?' asked Buddha.

The high priest was speechless with rage and tried to assault Buddha, shouting out 'How dare you say such things to me?'

But Bimbisara understood on which side lay the victory. He stopped the sacrifice, dismissed the high priest, and embraced Buddhism.

The Half Pomegranate

The Lord Buddha had announced that on a particular day he would receive alms with his own hands for the support of the poor and the unfortunate, and had begged all to come with whatever offerings they were pleased to give. On the appointed day, Buddha sat at Rajagriha in a conspicuous place and began receiving alms. First came King Bimbisara with gifts of lands, houses and other valuable properties with suitable endowments. Buddha received them with only one hand. After this, several nobles, merchants and other rich men offered their gifts to 'The Enlightened One' who received all of them with one hand. Then came a miserable-looking old woman with half a pomegranate in her hand. She saluted the world teacher and said, 'Lord, I heard about your receiving alms only now. I had eaten half a pomegranate and had only this half left. I have nothing else in this world to give, so I brought this. Be pleased to accept it.' Buddha stretched forth both his hands and accepted the half pomegranate. Bimbisara, Ajatasatru and the rest were astounded. 'Oh, Blessed One,' said Bimbisara, 'inscrutable are your ways. Why did you receive this shrunken half pomegranate with both your hands, whereas you received all our costly gifts only with one hand?' Buddha smiled and said, 'Oh King, you have given costly presents, but none of you gave a tenth of what you have, and this, too, you gave more for the sake of glory than from motives of real charity. This woman gave her all and gave it willingly. That explains my action.'

The Young Mother

One day, as Buddha was sitting under a banyan tree, a young woman went weeping to him with a dead child in her arms. 'Lord,' she said, 'my first born, my only child, is dead. Take pity on me and bring it back to life.' And she wept as if her heart would break. The Blessed One knew the futility of reasoning with her or teaching her the four great truths when she was in such a frame of mind. So he told her, 'Daughter, bring a handful of gingili seeds from a person none of whose relations have died, and I shall bring your child back to life.' The mother was overjoyed at this seemingly simple request. She put her dead child tenderly on the lap of the world teacher and went to the adjacent village. Her experience of the world was so small that she did not know the impossible nature of her quest. She went first to a house and knocked at the door. A young woman came. 'Will you please give me a handful of gingili seeds?' asked the mother. 'Most willingly,' said the other and brought a handful of gingili seeds. The mother took them and, as she was about to go, said casually, 'I hope none of your relations have ever died.' At that the other burst into a loud moan and said, 'Why do you rake up my unhealed wounds? Don't you know that my only brother died but a month ago and that my father died only a year back?' The young mother said, 'I am very sorry for you, but I don't want your gingili seeds.' She went to another house. She found an elderly woman there and asked for a handful of gingili seeds. The lady brought them. Before receiving them, the young mother asked, 'I hope none of your relatives have died?' On hearing this the other burst out into loud lamentations saying, 'My son, my only son, the boy whom I tended for twenty long years, he died six months ago. Who are you that remind me of my misery?' The young mother said, 'I am very sorry, but I do not want your gingili seeds.' She went to another house where she found a widow aged about sixty; she said to her 'Mother, give me a handful of gingili seeds if none of your relatives have died.' The old widow laughed and said, 'Daughter, I shall give you ten handfuls of gingili seeds if you want, but, of course, several of my relations have died. Why, my dear husband died thirty years ago. I felt it as an inconsolable loss then. But, now, I know that all this is inevitable, and don't feel so sorry. Unless people die, where would be the room in this world for all the babes that are born every day? The world will become overcrowded like Hell. Where is your father, his father, his father and so on? Some of these must assuredly have died. Death is the one universal event in the life of every man who is born.' The young mother felt how impossible her quest was and so returned to Buddha and told him about the fruitlessness of her search. 'Daughter,' said Gautama 'Nothing is permanent. Everything is subject to change, decay and death. Such change, decay and death cause sorrow and suffering. The only way to avoid them is to be unattached and to take them as natural phenomena and to take to the Aryan eightfold path which leads to the cessation of all pain and suffering.' 'Teach me that path,' said the mother. 'Go and bury your child and return.' She did as directed, learnt the four truths and at last became a celebrated nun.

Face Saving

Amritodana, the paternal uncle of Buddha, had a fine boy born on the same day as Rahula the son of Buddha. He named the boy Ananda (All-joy) as Kapilavastu was full of happy revelry that day, it being Holi or the anniversary of the burning of the God of Love by Siva, enraged at the interruption of his asceticism. Amritodana called an expert astrologer, and asked him to cast the boy's horoscope. He did so and said, 'Prince Ananda, born on the day celebrating the burning of the God of Love, will be devoid of lust and will become the personal attendant of the Lord Buddha, the sage of the Sakyas.' Amritodana did not like his boy to become a monk. So he watched him with zealous care.

When the boy grew up to be twenty, Amritodana took him away to Vaisali when Buddha went to Kapilavastu. When Buddha went to Vaisali, Amritodana hurried Ananda back to Kapilavastu. But once Buddha returned to Kapilavastu unexpectedly and sat on the verandah of Amritodana's house. Ananda opened the door and saw Buddha perspiring in that hot weather, and so at once took a fan and stood fanning him. The prophecy was fulfilled.

Then Buddha spoke to him about the four great truths, suffering, the cause of suffering, the cessation of suffering, and the noble eight-fold path. Ananda listened enraptured. When Buddha rose to go, Ananda followed him. Amritodana, coming out of his house, asked Ananda to return. 'No,' said Ananda, 'that is impossible. Excuse me, father, for my inability to obey you.' 'You cannot become a monk without my permission,' raged Amritodana. 'Then, father, give me your permission,' replied Ananda.

Just then, Suddhodana also came out of his house. He said to Amritodana, 'My son became an ascetic without my permission and despite every precaution of mine to prevent his doing so. Your son, too, will do so, whatever you do. So, why not regularise this and give him permission to become a monk, so that people may not say that all our sons are disobedient?' 'But, what good will such giving of permission do?' asked Amritodana. 'It will at least save our face,' answered Suddhodana. Amritodana was convinced by this argument and gave the necessary permission. Ananda was taken to the Nyagrodha Vihara on the morrow. In the presence of Amritodana and Suddhodana, he repeated to the venerable Dasabala Kasyapa, 'I seek refuge in the Buddha; I seek refuge in the order; I seek refuge in the Dharma,' and was then taken into the holy order. Thus was Amritodana's face saved.

Critics Silenced

When Buddha became fifty years old, he said to the Bhikshus, 'Bhikshus, I am bent down with age and infirmities and am worn out. Kindly appoint a Bhikshu to attend to my wants'. The venerable Kaundinya said, 'May the Blessed One accept me as an attendant!' 'You are too old, Oh Kaundinya. You yourself will require an attendant,' remonstrated Buddha. Asvajit, Subahu and the other senior disciples who volunteered were told the same thing by Buddha. Maudgalayana, who too had received a similar reply, thought that Ananda would be a fit person and would be sure to be approved by Buddha. So he and Sariputra went and asked Ananda if he would accept this most honourable place. Ananda at first refused. 'Venerable Sariputra,' said he, 'choose me not as the attendant of the Blessed One. It is as difficult to wait on him as to approach a mighty sixty-year old elephant of the Matanga forest, strong, with great curved tusks and deep chest, revelling in the fray.' Finally, he agreed on three conditions, namely, that he should never have to partake of the Blessed One's food , or to wear his underclothes or cloak, that he should not have to accompany the Blessed One when he went to a layman's house, and that he might, at any time he wanted, see and revere the Blessed One.

The great Buddha agreed to these conditions though he had rejected the offers of five hundred others who had offered to serve him unconditionally. The rejected ones asked him the reason.

He told them, 'His conditions are only signs of his humility. He is so humble that he does not feel himself worthy of partaking of the very meal I eat or of wearing clothes worn by me or of sitting and eating along with me at laymen's houses. He wants to approach me whenever he likes so that he may clear all his doubts.' The questioners, who numbered five hundred, were not satisfied. The wise Buddha saw this and took the five hundred with him wherever he went so that they might watch Ananda's behaviour and be convinced of his superiority to them.

Soon afterwards, Buddha went with Ananda and the other five hundred to Rajagriha. Devadatta, Buddha's cousin and arch-enemy, had, by a heavy bribe, induced the mahout of Ajatasatru to let loose the ferocious state elephant Ratnapala or Vasupala drunk with arrack, on Buddha and his party. The five hundred bhikshus fled helter skelter on seeing the elephant come along, leaving Buddha to his fate. Ananda alone stood by the Master. 'Ananda,' said Buddha 'why don't you run also?' 'I run, leaving the Blessed One!' said Ananda' 'No my place is with the Blessed One. Let those who want to run and save their skins, do so!' The great Buddha smiled. 'The ferocious elephant is coming, Ananda,' said he. 'I have taken refuge in the Buddha,' said Ananda. 'Let the Blessed One do what seems to him fit.' The elephant had by this time reached them. Buddha faced the elephant boldly and spoke a few coaxing words to it as he was in the habit of doing to his rogue elephants when he was the Prince at Kapilavastu. Ratnapala was subdued and followed Buddha to his stable quiet as a lamb. The Bhikshus who had fled saw this miracle, and sneaked back to Buddha. 'Bhadantas,[2]' said the Wise One, 'where had you been? Why did you not take Ananda with you?' They stood dumbfounded with shame and acknowledged that the preference of Ananda to them was only an act of justice.

War Prevented

The Sakyas of Kapilavastu and their neighbours, the Kolis of Koli, were separated by the river Rohini which some husbandmen on both sides had jointly bounded and from which they were irrigating the fields on the opposite banks. One year the water in the Rohini was very low due to the failure of rains, and the husbandmen on either side wanted to monopolise the little water that remained, to the exclusion of the other side. These few Koli and Sakya husbandmen exchanged words and then engaged in general abuse of the opposite tribe. More and more Sakyas sided with the Sakya husbandmen, and more and more Kolis with the Koli husbandmen in the quarrel, without knowing its origin. Finally, the entire tribes headed by their respective princes prepared for a war for vindicating national honour without the haziest notion of what it was all about. Just then, the great Buddha heard of this and hurried to the place. On seeing him, the Sakyas and the Kolis, who were all Buddhists, hid their arms and pretended to have simply assembled there for fun. Buddha asked them 'Brethren, have you assembled to celebrate the river goddess' festival?' They had then to tell him that they had assembled for a fight. 'Why?' asked the great Buddha. The princes did not know and could not tell. They asked the generals, who asked the captains, who asked the headmen. Finally, the two rival bands of husbandmen were produced, and they explained the cause. 'What is the price of water?' asked Buddha. 'Is it dearer than human blood?' 'Far cheaper,' said they, 'There is no comparison.' 'Then why shed precious human blood for worthless water?' asked Buddha. The husbandmen agreed thereafter to share the water alike, and the armies dispersed peacefully.

A Robber Reforms

Angulimala was a terrible brigand living in a forest between Ayodhya and Rajagriha. He used to be a terror to all passers-by. Those who had anything of value he would rob and kill. Those who had nothing he would kill just because they had nothing. Thousands of families held his name in execration for either father, brother, son, uncle or nephew killed by him. But they feared the man even more than they hated him and were powerless to take revenge.

One day, the great Buddha wanted to cross this forest in order to go from Ayodhya to Rajagriha. The citizens of Ayodhya implored him not to cross it but to take a round-about way. 'That wretch has no respect for monks and treats saints and sinners alike. Let not the Exalted One pass that way,' said they. The Buddha set out alone with Ananda, saying that this was too rare a chance to be missed. 'The worst sinner can be redeemed,' said he 'let me have a try.'

Buddha and Ananda soon entered the depths of the forest. Angulamala rushed at them with his club. 'Hand over whatever you have,' he roared, 'or be ready to die'. 'All that I have are the four truths: suffering, the cause of suffering, the cessation from suffering, and the noble eight-fold path', answered Buddha, 'and these will free a man from the chain of births and deaths. You are welcome to what I have.' 'I shall smash your brains for having nothing,' roared Angulamala. 'Are these gems of truth nothing to you, friend?' asked Buddha. 'Unlike the ordinary gems you get, they can be given to others without making you any poorer.' 'All this jargon will not avail you. Here, prepare yourself for death,' said the robber and raised his club. 'Friend,' said Buddha. 'I have come here from love for you. I do not fear you. Have you thought of what would become of you when you are too old to rob others? As long as your strength lasts, this profession of yours will appear attractive. but when age overtakes you, what will you do? When death claims you as a victim, do you know what will happen as the result of your sinful and cruel life? Hundreds of years in Hell. Why store up such horrible tortures for these ephemeral gains? Why not seek the peace which never leaves, the joy everlasting, by taking to honest living? Listen to the truths I have been preaching, and, if you are dissatisfied or unconvinced, then do as you like.' Angulamala agreed. Then Buddha preached to him the four great truths, the sadness of life, the sorrow which haunts man at every step, the roots of sorrow in lust, greed and anger, the cessation of sorrow by giving up this three-fold demon, and the noble eight-fold path. Angulamala listened with growing interest. As he heard, tears rolled down his cheeks. In the end, the robber sobbed like a child and fell at Buddha's feet and craved to be received into the order as a monk. The great Buddha did so and took him along with him. In some months he became a devout monk, following the tenets of Buddha to the very letter. The former votary of violence became an apostle of non-violence, and openly preached the practice of non-violence, under even the most provoking circumstances.

Some time after his conversion, Buddha took him to Rajagriha. The populace at first fled at the sight of the terrible brigand. But on seeing how gentle and non-violent he had become, they lost their fear of him entirely. Soon, news of his non-violence spread abroad, and the relatives of the victims of his former murders and rapine took courage to wreak their vengeance on him. Armed with clubs they fell on him in hundreds in the streets of Rajagriha and beat him all over the body, at first hesitatingly from fear of retaliation, and later with the accumulated rancour of years. Soon Angulamala's head and body were bleeding profusely. He went to Buddha, with his bleeding injuries. 'Suffer it patiently, brother,' said Buddha, to him, 'you are now paying for your past *karma* which might have cost you centuries of suffering in purgatory. Now, do you see what sufferings your former victims must have endured at your hands?'

Just then, a further batch of men rushed to attack Angulamala and finish him off. 'Friends,' said Buddha to them. 'Why do you attack this man who has reformed and accumulate bad *karma* for yourself?' 'A robber can never reform,' said they. 'He has reformed. It seems to me that it is the citizens who cannot reform,' replied the great Buddha. They felt ashamed and went their way.

Caste at Source

The great Buddha was one day stopping at Ikkhanankala village in Kosala. That village had been given away as a grant with all feudal rights to the Brahmin Pokkharasadi by Prasenajit of Kosala. On hearing that Buddha was camping in his village, Pokkharasadi called his chief disciple Ambattha and told him, 'The Buddha is camping in our village. He is said to be a fully awakened one with the 32 signs of a great man. Go and verify it and then come and tell me. If he is, as rumour has it, really a Great One, I want to meet him.'

Ambattha set out with a dozen Brahmins to meet Buddha. He was learned in the Vedas but was a conceited young man full of caste arrogance. He did not think that a Kshatriya like Buddha could teach anything to Brahmins who had emerged from the mouth of Brahma himself. He had consented to meet Buddha only in obedience to the orders of Pokkharasadi whom he dared not disobey.

Ambattha and his Brahmin comrades reached the grove where the rest-house was. Buddha's disciples said to Ambattha, 'There, Ambattha, is his lodging where the door is shut. Go quietly up and enter the porch silently and then give a cough and knock. The Blessed One will open the door for you.' Ambattha did so. The Blessed One opened the door. Ambattha and the other young Brahmins went in. The Blessed one sat down. Ambattha's friends also sat down on one side after saluting him.

Ambattha kept walking about and fidgeting and standing in front of the Great One. 'Ambattha,' asked the Buddha 'Is that the way to hold conversations with aged teachers, teachers of your teachers—standing like that and moving about disrespectfully while they are sitting?' 'No,' said Ambattha, 'If the teachers were Brahmins, I should sit if they were sitting, stand if they were standing, recline if they were reclining, walk if they were walking. But with shavelings, sham friars, low-born Sakyas, these rules of etiquette need not be followed. I can do just what I please. That is why I am behaving like this.' The other Brahmins giggled. 'Ambattha,' said Buddha, 'what have the Sakyas done to you?' 'They were sitting in their council hall when I went there. They continued sitting without rising to honour me. They just motioned me to a seat, those low-born menials. When I got angry, they joked at my expense, those low-born menials.' 'And, may I know what family you belong to?' asked Buddha. 'I am a Kanhayana,' said Ambattha with pride. 'Do you know that the Kanhayanas are ultimately descended from one of the Sakyas, one of the low-born menials you despise, by a slave girl?' asked the Buddha. Ambattha remained silent but furious. His Brahmin friends said to Buddha, 'Let not the Blessed One insult Ambattha. He is a Brahmin of good descent well-learned in the Vedas and the chief disciple of the great Brahmin Pokkharasadi'. 'Friends,' said Buddha 'if he is really learned he can reply for himself. Ambattha, what have you heard from learned Brahmins well stricken in years about the origin of the Kanhayanas? Didn't they tell you that they are all descended from a Sakya noble by a slave girl at the court of the great king Okaka? Reply, friend, and prove that you are really a Brahmin worthy of being a disciple of the great Brahmin Pokkharasadi.' Ambattha still remained silent. 'Speak, Ambattha,' said the great Buddha, 'else, may your head split into eight pieces for suppressing the truth.' Ambattha said slowly. 'The Brahmins well stricken in year have told me the same thing, namely that the Kanhayanas are descended from Kanha who was born to a Sakya by the slave girl Disa.' 'Ah,' said his Brahmin friends, 'what fools we were to have served this base-born slave girl's child!' 'Say not so, sirs,' said Buddha, 'that slave girl's son Kanha was one of the greatest sages who lived. He went to the Deccan and learnt many occult arts and mysteries. Then he went to King Okaka and demanded his daughter in marriage. Okaka, indignant at a slave's child demanding his daughter in marriage, took his bow and fixed an arrow to it and aimed it at Kanha. But such was Kanha's miraculous power that the arrow would not go. Nor could Okaka take away his hand from the bow. Finally, the nobles and people entreated Kanha to have pity on the king, and Kanha asked him to discharge the arrow on his heir, promising that no harm would ensue. Trembling, and with terror freezing his soul, Okaka discharged the arrow at his heir. Lo! the arrow disappeared into him without doing the least harm. Then Okaka gave his daughter in marriage to Kanha. The Kanhayanas are the descendants from that union. So despise not Kanha or the Kanhayanas.' The young Brahmins stopped laughing at Ambattha. Ambattha too saw the ridiculousness of his caste arrogance and so saluted the great Buddha and sat on one side reverently and discussed with him. Buddha's tracing his caste to its source had the marvellous effect of taking away his arrogance and putting some sense into him. He saw the thirty-two signs of a great man in Buddha and went and reported this to Pokkharasadi. He also related the story of his initial insolence and the way in which it was set right. Pokkharasadi was furious at his disciple's insult to the great Buddha. He kicked him over and over again, shouting, 'You dullard! You idiot! You are a disgrace to teachers! You conceited pup! I must go and apologise to Buddha on your behalf.' That day it was too late. The next day he went and prostrated himself before Buddha and said, 'He is young and foolish, Gotama, that young Brahmin Ambattha. Forgive him, Gotama.' 'Let him be quite happy, Brahmin, that young Brahmin Ambattha,' said Buddha. 'I have forgiven him already and convinced him of the folly of putting trust in lineage or taking pride in birth and told him that he who is perfect in wisdom and righteousness is the best among gods and men.' 'That is right,' said Pokkharasadi. 'There is nothing like tracing caste to its source and following it to its origin to convince a silly fool like him.'

Beauty Analysed

Subha, a beautiful nun of 22, was walking in Jivaka's mango grove. A libertine prince went to her and exclaimed, 'What a pretty maid you are! Why should you be a nun? Cast off that yellow robe and come with me and know the joys of love. There is a pleasant breeze blowing. Birds are singing. Let us go to yonder pleasure park, sport in that lotus pond together and have a heart to heart talk. I shall give you a palace to live in, scores of maidservants and the finest Benares silks and the most exquisite food.' 'Go away,' said she. 'I have received initiation at the hands of the great Buddha and become passionless and pure. Turbid is your mind. I have no turbidity. I am free from desire or the lust for enjoyment. Go.' 'Oh, this beauty of yours should not be wasted in a monastery. You fair ones are meant to live in a palace, sleeping on soft beds, bathing in scented water. Oh, gazelle-eyed one, I shall willingly give my whole life to have a single look at your eyes. Those bewitching eyes of yours will always be haunting me. What would I not give to gaze at them always?' 'What are they but balls of flesh, blood and brine? Why do you get so passionate about them?' asked Subha. 'Flesh, blood, or brine, I want them, I hunger for them more than I do for Heaven,' said he. 'Then have one and make merry' said she gouging out an eye and handing it over to him, streaming with blood and brine. The rake was astounded and shocked, and shrank from that bleeding ball which was her eye.

He fell at her feet and said 'Sister, pardon me, I never thought you meant it all.' 'Buddha's daughter never lies,' said she. The prince then went to the Buddha, told him they story, and implored him to restore they eye which the Blessed One did by virtue of his *iddhis*.'

Gold is Cheap, Great Men Scarce

Ambapali was a famous dancing girl of Vaisali. She was renowned for her beauty, and lived in a luxurious villa in the midst of a mango grove surrounded by a magnificent park. Kings, princes and citizens alike eagerly solicited her favours. King Bimbisara of Magadha was one of her lovers. During one of his visits, he spoke to her of the great Buddha. 'He left a wife more beautiful than you, he left a kingdom vaster than Vaisali, he abandoned his only son, he forsook the finest food and clothes, all so that he may find a solution for birth, disease, old age and death, and rid the world of sorrow. His love was so very great,' said he. 'What is his love like? It must be very different from yours,' she asked. 'Of course,' said Bimbisara 'My love is selfish, but his is unselfish.

His the fire that warms but does not burn
His the mind that acts but does not yearn
His the heart that loves but does not lust
His the faith that lives but does not crust.'

Ambapali listened with rapt attention and resolved to see the Exalted One.

So when the great Buddha was proceeding to Vaisali one day, she met him on the way. At the very sight of his radiant face, replete with holiness, and his eyes full of love, sympathy, understanding and pity, she thought of the contrast between her evil living and his holy life. Prostrating before him, she invited him to the midday meal at her place next day if the holy one would deign to do so. The Exalted One signified his assent, as usual, by his silence. Thereupon Ambapali left.

Some ten minutes after she had left, the supreme magistrates and rulers of Vaisali went in their silk robes and gold palanquins to the Blessed One and invited him to the midday meal with them the next day. The great Buddha replied, 'I have already accepted another invitation.' 'Whose?' asked they in surprise. 'Ambapali's,' said he. 'What! The courtesan's! The mango girl's!' cried the magistrates. How can the holy one go to a dancing girl's house?' 'No one has more need of holiness than she,' said the Buddha. 'But, surely, our invitation ought to take precedence over hers,' said they. 'I don't recognize lay distinctions,' replied Buddha. 'The invitation accepted by me first takes precedence over all the others.' 'Suppose we persuade her to waive her right for tomorrow in our favour?' asked they. 'If she, of her own accord, agrees, you are free to do so,' replied the Buddha.

The magistrates hastened to Ambapali's mango grove shouting, 'The mango girl shall not get the better of us!' They said to her 'Waive your right tomorrow. Let us have the honour of entertaining the Exalted One first.' 'No,' said she, 'I got him, and I shall keep him.' 'We shall give you a thousand gold pieces,' said they. 'Not for a million gold pieces will I agree to give him up,' she replied, 'Gold is cheap, but great men are scarce.' 'What do you mean?' asked they. 'Men have come in hundreds to seek my favours—kings, princes and millionaires. Hankering after my body, they came scattering their gold about to my maidservants' maidservants. What do I care for gold or gems? I am surfeited with them. Here is a gem of a man, the jewel in the lotus, come hankering after my soul and caring not for my body. Shall I leave him to you men of vanity? I know you all. Not one of you but has fawned at my feet. Threaten me not, nor cry out.' 'The mango girl has got the better of us!' 'This is not the first time the mango girl has got the better of you; this is only the first time somebody has got the better of the mango girl. Tomorrow I shall have the Blessed One for myself.'

The magistrates went back to Buddha disappointed. 'She refused to waive her right,' said they. 'I thought as much,' said Buddha, 'now I have every hope of converting her.'

The next day Ambapali entertained the great Buddha and his monks most sumptuously. After the Holy One had washed his bowl and hands, and sat down, she prostrated herself before him and sat down reverently on one side and requested for instruction in the great truths. The Exalted One taught her. She was converted and became a nun, and gave the magnificent park, mango grove and villa to the Order.

The Greatest Teacher Ever

The great Buddha was camping in the Pavarika mango grove shortly before his death. His famous disciple, the venerable Sariputra, went and saluted him and took his seat respectfully by his side saying, 'Oh Exalted One, Thou art the greatest teacher ever born. There never was in the past, there is not now, and there never will be in the future a teacher to equal Thee.' 'Grand are your words, Oh Sariputra, and bold beyond compare,' said Buddha. 'Why, you burst forth into a veritable rhapsody. Of course, you must have known all the Exalted Ones of the past ages and gauged with your mind their mode of life, wisdom and conduct and degree of enlightenment and emancipation.' 'Oh, no,' replied Sariputra. 'You must have perceived all the Exalted Ones who shall be born in the long ages to come and gauged with your mind their mode of life, wisdom and conduct and degree of enlightenment and emancipation!' said the Buddha. 'Oh, no, Lord,' replied Sariputra. 'But, at least, you have penetrated my mind fully with yours and gauged my mode of life, wisdom and conduct and degree of enlightenment and emancipation,' said the Buddha. 'Not even that, Lord,' said Sariputra. 'Then, Sariputra, why burst forth into such a song of grand and bold words, why hail me as the greatest teacher ever?'

The Evil One Conquers At last

Soon after Buddha attained *Nirvana*, he felt death come over him. Mara, the Evil One, said to him, 'Pass away now, Lord. Let the Exalted One die now as he has attained Nirvana than which there is nothing higher.' 'No, Mara, I do not want to die a *pratyeka* Buddha, saving myself alone and not helping others to save themselves. I will not die till I have taught men and women the great truths which I have realized, and enabled them to grasp them and explain and propagate them and save those who take heed,' said Buddha. 'Nobody in the world wants your hard and thorny path,' said Mara. 'They want an easy all-giving God who can be flattered by hymns or sacrifices and made to give salvation, or a gross materialism indulging in the delights of the senses. So, why worry about them?' 'No, Mara, you are wrong. I, too, thought like that at first and said to myself, 'Will the world, so much enveloped in sensuality and pleasure, receive this message of self-discipline and abandonment of useless living? Would it not be well if I pass away without putting myself to inconvenience?' But the God Brahma himself came to me and asked me to proclaim my doctrines to the world as there were persons ready to listen to my message. So, get thee gone,' said Buddha, and, with a supreme exercise of will, overcame impending death.

Forty-four years afterwards, when Buddha had initiated and trained thousands of monks and nuns, and had hundreds of thousands of lay followers, he again felt death approaching. Mara once more approached the Blessed One. 'Pass away, now, Lord. Let the Exalted One die now,' said he. 'The great truths have been sufficiently proclaimed.' 'No, Mara, I will not die till I have taught the monks and nuns and lay followers all the truths so minutely that they will be able to combat all schism and heresy. So long as my *bhikshus* want me, I shall live on enlightening them,' said Buddha. 'Then, promise me Lord that when Ananda, the *bhikshu* who loves the Exalted One most, neglects to request the Blessed One to live on despite sixteen different hints, the Blessed One will consent to die.' 'I promise that, Oh Evil One,' Buddha promised.

Shortly after this, Buddha was at Vulture's Peak at Rajagriha with Ananda. He praised the beauty of the scenery there and told Ananda that he had thoroughly practised and developed the *iddhis* and could therefore, should he desire it, live on yet for an aeon or for the portion of the aeon which yet remained. Ananda did not take the obvious hint and request him to live on for an aeon for the good and happiness of the masses, out of pity for the world and for the good of gods and men. Buddha repeated the hint at the banyan grove, Robbers' Cliff, Sattapanni Cave, Black Rock, Sitavana Cave, the tapoda grove, the bamboo grove, the mango grove and the deer forest at Rajagriha, but Ananda did not take the hint and make the request.

Buddha was now turning eighty. When camping at Beluva, he had gripping pains due to dysentery and felt death approaching once more. He said to himself 'I will not die yet. The congregation of *bhikshus* is scattered and it will not be right for me to pass away now without addressing my disciples, without taking leave of the Order.' So he again overcame death by the exercise of his willpower.

Ananda was overjoyed at the Exalted One's sudden and unexpected recovery from dysentery and said to him, 'My body became weak like a creeper, the horizon became invisible, I forgot all that I learnt, forgot even the four directions and the days of the week on seeing the Blessed One sinking. My only hope was that the Blessed One would not pass away till at least he had left some instructions about the Order.' 'Ananda, the Tathagatha has not got the closed fist of the teacher. I have taught you everything and concealed nothing. I am turning eighty years of age, and just as a worn-out cart, Ananda, can be kept going only with the help of thongs, so, methinks, the body of the Tathagatha can only be kept going by bandaging it up. Oh Ananda, when I am gone, be ye lamps unto yourselves. Be ye a refuge to yourselves. Betake yourselves to no external refuge. Hold fast to the truth as a lamp. Hold fast as a refuge to the Truth. Look not for refuge to anyone beside yourselves. Look upon your body, feelings, moods, ideas, and remain strenuous, self-possessed, and mindful, having overcome both the hankering and the dejection common in the world. Thus will you reach the summit of achievement; thus will you attain the summit of detachment, where the body, not attached to any outward things, become splunged by the cessation of any separate sensation in that concentration of the heart which is not concerned with any material object. Then your body will be at ease, and Nirvana will be near.'

Later on, the great Buddha and Ananda went to Vaisali. There at the Udena shrine, Gotamuka shrine, shrine of seven mangoes, at the Bahuputra shrine, at the Sarandada shrine and at the Chapala shrine, Buddha told Ananda how beautiful Vaisali was and how handsome the shrines were and repeated the information regarding his having so thoroughly developed his *iddhis* that he could, if he desired, prolong his life for an aeon or the remaining portion of the aeon. Still Ananda did not take the hint and request him to live on for the remaining portion of the aeon for the good of the masses. Mara had possessed him and made him oblivious to the hints. The sixteenth hint at the Chapala shrine having thus failed to elicit the necessary request, Buddha told Ananda, 'You may leave me, Ananda, and do whatever, now seemeth to thee fit.' 'So be it, Lord,' said Ananda, who left him and sat under a tree close by.

Mara then approached Buddha and said 'Pass away, now, lord, according to your promise. Let the Exalted One die now.' Buddha said, 'Oh, Evil One, make thyself happy. The death of the Tathagatha shall take place before long. At the end of three months from this time, the Tathagatha will pass away.' So Mara departed happy.

Ananda then approached Buddha and was told about the surrender of the remaining portion of his life. 'Three months hence, the Tathagatha will utterly pass away.' Ananda wept bitter tears and said, 'I implore the Blessed One to live on for an aeon or at least for the remaining portion of the aeon for the good of the world.' 'Too late, now, oh Ananda,' said the Tathagatha and told him the whole history, ending, 'Thine is the fault, thine the offence.' Ananda rolled on the ground, crying out bitterly. 'Too soon will the Exalted One pass away. Too soon will the happy one pass away. Too soon the light will go out of the world. Then will there be terror, then will the hair stand on end, when he, endowed with every grace, the supreme Buddha, dies. Oh, exalted one, for the sake of Ananda, live on for at least the remaining portion of the aeon.' 'That is impossible,' said Buddha. 'I have already surrendered the remaining portion of my life to Mara. The Tathagatha will not go back on his word.'

Ananda continued to roll on the ground with grief. The great Buddha lifted him up and said, 'Do not grieve, oh Ananda. It is in the very nature of all things near and dear unto us that we must be prepared to leave them, part from them sever ourselves from them. How can anything born and brought into being, and containing in itself the seeds of its dissolution, go on forever, and not be dissolved?'

Finding a New Spring

Once upon a time a certain tradesman was leading a caravan to another country to sell his goods. Along the way they came to the edge of a severe hot-sand desert. They asked about, and found that during the day time the sun heats up the fine sand until it's as hot as charcoal, so no one can walk on it—not even bullocks or camels! So the caravan leader hired a desert guide, one who could follow the stars, so they could travel only at night when the sand cools down. They began the dangerous night-time journey across the desert.

A couple of nights later, after eating their evening meal, and waiting for the sand to cool, they started out again. Later that night, the desert guide, who was driving the first cart, saw from the stars that they were getting close to the other side of the desert. He had also overeaten, so that when he relaxed, he dozed off to sleep. Then the bullocks who, of course, couldn't tell directions by reading the stars, gradually turned to the side and went in a big wide circle until they ended up at the same place they had started from!

By then it was morning, and the people realized they were back at the same spot they'd camped at the day before. They lost heart and began to cry about their condition. Since the desert crossing was supposed to be over by now, they had no more water and were afraid they would die of thirst. They even began to blame the caravan leader and the desert guide. 'We can do nothing without water!' they complained.

Then the tradesman thought to himself, 'If I lose courage now, in the middle of this disastrous situation, my leadership has no meaning. If I fall to weeping and regretting this misfortune, and do nothing, all these goods and bullocks and even the lives of the people, including myself, may be lost. I must be energetic and face the situation!' So he began walking back and forth, trying to think out a plan to save them all.

Remaining alert, out of the corner of his eye, he noticed a small clump of grass. He thought, 'Without water, no plant could live in this desert.' So he called over the most energetic of his fellow travellers and asked them to dig up the ground on that very spot. They dug and dug, and after a while they got down to a large stone. Seeing it they stopped, and began to blame the leader again, saying 'This effort is useless. We're just wasting our time!' But the tradesman replied, 'No no, my friends, if we give up the effort we will all be ruined and our poor animals will die. Let us be encouraged!'

As he said this, he got down into the hole, put his ear to the stone, and heard the sound of flowing water. Immediately, he called over a boy who had been digging and said, 'If you give up, we will all perish, so take this heavy hammer and strike the rock.'

The boy lifted the hammer over his head and hit the rock as hard as he could, and he himself was the most surprised when the rock split in two and a mighty flow of water gushed out from under it! All the people were overjoyed. They drank and bathed and washed the animals and cooked their food and ate.

Before they left, they raised a high banner so that other

travellers could see it from afar and come to the new spring in the middle of the hot-sand desert. Then they continued on safely to the end of their journey.

The moral is: Don't give up too easily, keep on trying until you reach the goal.

The Golden Plate

Once upon a time in a place called Seri, there were two salesmen of pots and pans and hand-made trinkets. They agreed to divide the town between them. They also said that after one had gone through his area, it was all right for the other to try and sell where the first had already been.

One day, while one of them was coming down a street, a poor little girl saw him and asked her grandmother to buy her a bracelet. The old grandmother replied, 'How can we poor people buy bracelets?' The little girl said, 'Since we don't have any money, we can give our black sooty old plate.' The old woman agreed to give it a try, so she invited the dealer inside.

The salesman saw that these people were very poor and innocent, so he didn't want to waste his time with them. Even though the old woman pleaded with him, he said he had no bracelet that she could afford to buy. Then she asked, 'We have an old plate that is useless to us, can we trade it for a bracelet?' The man took it and, while examining it, happened to scratch the bottom of it. To his surprise, he saw that underneath the black soot, it was a golden plate! But he didn't let on that he had noticed it. Instead he decided to deceive these poor people so he could get the plate for next to nothing. He said, 'This is not worth even one bracelet. There's no value in this. I don't want it!' He left, thinking he would return later when they would accept even less for the plate.

Meanwhile the other salesman, after finishing in his part of town, followed after the first as they had agreed. He ended up at the same house. Again the poor little girl begged her grandmother to trade the old plate for a bracelet. The woman saw that this was a nice tender looking merchant and thought, 'He's a good man, not like the rough-talking first salesman.' So she invited him in and offered to trade the same black sooty old plate for one bracelet. When he examined it, he too saw that it was pure gold under the grime. He said to the old woman, 'All my goods and all my money together are not worth as much as this rich golden plate!'

Of course the woman was shocked at this discovery, but now she knew that he was indeed a good and honest fellow. So she said she would be glad to accept whatever he could trade for it. The salesman said, 'I'll give you all my pots and pans and trinkets, plus all my money, if you will let me keep just eight coins and my balancing scale, with its cover to put the golden plate in.' They made the trade. He went down to the river, where he paid the eight coins to the ferry man to take him across.

By then the greedy salesman had returned, already adding up huge imaginary profits in his head. When he met the little girl and her grandmother again, he said he had changed his mind and was willing to offer a few cents, but not one of his bracelets, for the useless black sooty old plate. The old woman then calmly told him of the trade she had just made with the honest salesman, and said, 'Sir, you lied to us.'

The greedy salesman was not ashamed of his lies, but he was saddened as he thought, 'I've lost the golden plate that must be worth a hundred thousand.' So he asked the woman, 'Which way did he go?' She told him the direction. He left all his things right there at her door and ran down to the river, thinking, 'He robbed me! He robbed me! He won't make a fool out of me!'

From the riverside he saw the honest salesman still crossing over on the ferry boat. He shouted to the ferry man, 'Come back!' But the good merchant told him to keep on going to the other side, and that's what he did.

Seeing that he could do nothing, the greedy salesman exploded with rage. He jumped up and down, beating his chest. He became so filled with hatred towards the honest man, who had won the golden plate, that he made himself cough up blood. He had a heart attack and died on the spot!

The moral is: Honesty is the best policy.

The Mouse Merchant

Once upon a time, an important adviser to a certain king was on his way to a meeting with the king and other advisers. Out of the corner of his eye, he saw a dead mouse by the roadside. He said to those who were with him. 'Even from such small beginnings as this dead mouse, an energetic young fellow could build a fortune. If he worked hard and used his intelligence, he could start a business and support a wife and family.'

A passerby heard the remark. He knew this was a famous adviser to the king, so he decided to follow his words. He picked up the dead mouse by the tail and went off with it. As luck would have it, before he had gone even a block, a shopkeeper stopped him. He said, 'My cat has been pestering me all morning. I'll give you two copper coins for that mouse.' So it was done.

With the two copper coins, he bought sweet cakes, and waited by the side of the road with them and some water. As he expected, some people who picked flowers for making garlands were returning from work. Since they were all hungry and thirsty, they agreed to buy sweet cakes and water for the price of a bunch of flowers from each of them. In the evening, the man sold the flowers in the city. With some of the money he bought more sweet cakes and returned the next day to sell to the flower pickers.

This went on for a while, until one day there was a terrible storm, with heavy rains and high winds. While walking by the king's pleasure garden, he saw that many branches had been blown off the trees and were lying all around. So he told the king's gardener that he would clear it all away for him, if he could keep the branches. The lazy gardener quickly agreed.

The man found some children playing in a park across the street. They were glad to collect all the branches at the entrance to the pleasure garden, for the price of just one sweet cake for each child.

Along came the king's potter, who was always on the lookout for firewood for his glazing oven. When he saw the piles of wood the children had just collected, he paid the man a handsome price for it. He even threw into the bargain some of his pots.

With his profits from selling the flowers and the firewood, the man opened up a refreshment shop. One day all the local grass mowers, who were on their way into town, stopped in his shop. He gave them free sweet cakes and drinks. They were surprised at his generosity and asked, 'What can we do for you?' He said there was nothing for them to do now, but he would let them know in the future.

A week later, he heard that a horse dealer was coming to the city with 500 horses to sell. So he got in touch with the grass mowers and told each of them to give him a bundle of grass. He told them not to sell any grass to the horse dealer until he had sold his. In this way he got a very good price.

Time passed until one day, in his refreshment shop, some customers told him that a new ship from a foreign country had just anchored in the port. He saw this to be the opportunity he had been waiting for. He thought and thought until he came up with a good business plan.

First, he went to a jeweller friend of his and paid a low price for a very valuable gold ring with a beautiful red ruby in it.

He knew that the foreign ship was from a country that had no rubies of its own, where gold too was expensive. So he gave the wonderful ring to the captain of the ship as an advance on his commission. To earn this commission, the captain agreed to send all his passengers to him as a broker. He would then lead them to the best shops in the city. In turn, the man got the merchants to pay him a commission for sending customers to them.

Acting as a middle man in this way, after several ships came into port, the man became very rich. Being pleased with his success, he also remembered that it had all started with the words of the king's wise adviser. So he decided to give him a gift of 100,000 gold coins. This was half his entire wealth. After making the proper arrangements, he met with the king's adviser and gave him the gift, along with his humble thanks.

The adviser was amazed, and he asked, 'How did you earn so much wealth to afford such a generous gift?' The man told him it had all started with the adviser's own words not so long ago. They had led him to a dead mouse, a hungry cat, sweet cakes, bunches of flowers, storm-damaged tree branches, children in the park, the king's potter, a refreshment shop, grass for 500 horses, a golden ruby ring, good business contacts, and finally, a large fortune.

Hearing all this, the royal adviser thought to himself, 'It would not be good to lose the talents of such an energetic man. I, too, have much wealth, as well as my beloved only daughter. As this man is single, he deserves to marry her. Then he can inherit my wealth in addition to his own, and my daughter will be well cared for.'

All this came to pass, and after the wise adviser died, the one who had followed his advice became the richest man in the city. The king appointed him to the adviser's position. Throughout his remaining life, he generously gave his money for the happiness and wellbeing of many people.

The moral is: With energy and ability, great wealth comes even from small beginnings.

The Price Maker

Long ago and far away, there was a king who ruled in Benares, in northern India. One of his ministers was called the Royal Price Maker, and he was a very honest man. His job was to set a fair price for anything the king wanted to buy or sell.

On some occasions, the king did not like his price making. He did not get as big a profit as he wanted. He did not want to pay so much when he bought, or sold for what he thought was not enough. So he decided to change the price maker.

One day he saw a nice-looking young man and he thought, 'This fellow will be good for my price-making position.' So he dismissed his honest price maker, and appointed this man to be the new one. The man thought, 'I must make the king happy by buying at very low prices and selling at very high prices.' So he made the prices ridiculous, without caring at all what anything was worth. This gained the greedy king a lot of money, and made him very happy. Meanwhile, all the others who dealt with the new price maker, including the king's other ministers and ordinary people, became very unhappy.

Then one day a horse merchant arrived in Benares with 500 horses to sell. There were stallions, mares and colts. The king invited the merchant to the palace, and called upon his Royal Price Maker to set a price for all 500 horses. Thinking only of pleasing the king, he said, 'The entire herd of horses is worth one cup of rice.' So the king ordered that one cup of rice be paid to the horse dealer, and all the horses were taken to the royal stables.

Of course the merchant was very upset, but he could do nothing at the moment. Later he heard about the former price maker, who had a reputation for being very fair and honest. So he approached him and told him what had happened. He wanted to hear his opinion, in order to get a proper price from the king. The former price maker said, 'If you do as I say, the king will be convinced of the true value of the horses. Go back to the price maker and satisfy him with a valuable gift. Ask him to tell the value of one cup of rice, in the presence of the king. If he agrees, come and tell me. I will go with you to the king.'

Following this advice, the merchant went to the price maker and gave him a valuable gift. The gift made him very happy, and he saw the value of pleasing the horse dealer. Then the merchant said to him, 'I was very happy with your previous evaluation. Can you please convince the king of the value of one cup of rice?' The foolish price maker said, 'Why not? I will explain the worth of one cup of rice, even in the presence of the king.'

So the price maker thought the horse dealer was satisfied with his cup of rice. He arranged for another meeting with the king, as the merchant was departing for his own country. The merchant reported back to the old price maker, and they went together to see the king.

All the king's ministers and his full court were in the royal meeting hall. The horse merchant said to the king, 'My lord, I understand that in this your country, my whole herd of 500 horses is worth one cup of rice. Before I leave for home, I want to know the value of one cup of rice in your country.' The king turned to his loyal price maker and said, 'What is the value of one cup of rice?'

The foolish price maker, in order to please the king, had

previously priced the herd of horses at one cup of rice. Now, after receiving a bribe from the horse dealer, he wanted to please him too. So he replied to the king, in his most dignified manner, 'Your worship, one cup of rice is worth the city of Benares, including even your own harem, as well as all the suburbs of the city. In other words, it is worth the whole kingdom of Benares!'

On hearing this, the royal ministers and wise men in the assembly hall started to roar with laughter, slapping their sides with their hands. When they calmed down a little, they said, 'Earlier we heard that the kingdom was priceless. Now we hear that all Benares, with its palaces and mansions, is worth only a cup of rice! The decision of the Royal Price Maker is so strange! Where did your highness find such a man? He is good only for pleasing a king such as you, not for making fair prices for a merchant who sells his horses from country to country.'

Hearing the laughter of his whole court, and the words of his ministers and advisers, the king was ashamed. So he brought back his former price maker to his official position. He agreed to a new fair price for the herd of horses, as set by the honest price maker. Having learned a lesson, the king and his kingdom lived justly and prospered.

The moral is: A fool in high office can bring shame even to a king.

Little Prince No-father

Once upon a time, the King of Benares went on a picnic in the forest. The beautiful flowers and trees and fruits made him very happy. As he was enjoying their beauty, he slowly went deeper and deeper into the forest. Before long, he became separated from his companions and realized that he was all alone.

Then he heard the sweet voice of a young woman. She was singing as she collected firewood. To keep from being afraid of being alone in the forest, the king followed the sound of the lovely voice. When he finally came upon the singer of the songs, he saw that she was a beautiful fair young woman, and immediately fell in love with her. They became very friendly, and the king became the father of the firewood woman's child.

Later, he explained how he had gotten lost in the forest, and convinced her that he was indeed the King of Benares. She gave him directions for getting back to his palace. The king gave her his valuable signet ring, and said, 'If you give birth to a baby girl, sell this ring and use the money to bring her up well. If our child turns out to be a baby boy, bring him to me along with this ring for recognition.' So saying, he departed for Benares.

In the fullness of time, the firewood woman gave birth to a cute little baby boy. Being a simple shy woman, she was afraid to take him to the fancy court in Benares, but she saved the king's signet ring.

In a few years, the baby grew into a little boy. When he played with the other children in the village, they teased him and mistreated him, and even started fights with him. It was because his mother was not married that the other children picked on him. They yelled at him, 'No-father! No-father! Your name should be No-father!'

Of course this made the little boy feel ashamed and hurt and sad. He often ran home crying to his mother. One day, he told her how the other children called him, 'No-father! No-father! Your name should be No-father!' Then his mother said, 'Don't be ashamed, my son. You are not just an ordinary little boy. Your father is the King of Benares!'

The little boy was very surprised. He asked his mother, 'Do you have any proof of this?' So she told him about his father giving her the signet ring, and that if the baby was a boy she should bring him to Benares, along with the ring as proof. The little boy said, 'Let's go then.' Because of what happened, she agreed, and the next day they set out for Benares.

When they arrived at the king's palace, the gate keeper told the king the firewood woman and her little son wanted to see him. They went into the royal assembly hall, which was filled with the king's ministers and advisers. The woman reminded the king of their time together in the forest. Finally she said, 'Your majesty, here is your son.'

The king was ashamed in front of all the ladies and gentlemen of his court. So, even though he knew the woman spoke the truth, he said, 'He is not my son!' Then the lovely young mother showed the signet ring as proof.

Again the king was ashamed and denied the truth, saying, 'It is not my ring!'

Then the poor woman thought to herself, 'I have no witness and no evidence to prove what I say. I have only my faith in the power of truth.' So she said to the king, 'If I throw this little boy up into the air, if he truly is your son, may he remain in the air without falling. If he is not your son, may he fall to the floor and die!'

Suddenly, she grabbed the boy by his foot and threw him up into the air. Lo and behold, the boy sat in the cross-legged position, suspended in mid-air, without falling. Everyone was astonished, to say the least! Remaining in the air, the little boy spoke to the mighty king. 'My lord, I am indeed a son born to you. You take care of many people who are not related to you. You even maintain countless elephants, horses and other animals. And yet, you do not think of looking after and raising me, your own son. Please do take care of me and my mother.'

Hearing this, the king's pride was overcome. He was humbled by the truth of the little boy's powerful words. He held out his arms and said, 'Come to me my son, and I will take good care of you.'

Amazed by such a wonder, all the others in the court put out their arms. They too asked the floating little boy to come to them. But he went directly from mid-air into his father's arms. With his son seated on his lap, the king announced that he would be the crown prince, and his mother would be the number one queen.

In this way, the king and all his court learned the power of truth. Benares became known as a place of honest justice. In time, the king died. The grown up crown prince wanted to show the people that all deserve respect, regardless of birth. So he had himself crowned under the official name, 'King No-father!' He went on to rule the kingdom in a generous and righteous way.

The moral is: The truth is always stronger than a lie.

The One-hundredth Prince

Once upon a time, there was a king who had one-hundred sons. The youngest, the one-hundredth, was Prince Gamani. He was very energetic, patient and kind.

All the princes were sent to be taught by teachers. Prince Gamani, even though he was the one-hundredth in line to the throne, was lucky enough to have the best teacher. He had the most learning and was the wisest of them of all. He was like a father to Prince Gamani, who liked, respected and obeyed him.

In those days, it was the custom to send each educated prince to a different province. There he was to develop the country and help the people. When Prince Gamani was old enough for this assignment, he went to his teacher and asked which province he should request. He said, 'Do not select any province. Instead, tell your father the king that if he sends you, his one-hundredth son, out to a province, there will be no son remaining to serve him in his home city.' Prince Gamani obeyed his teacher, and pleased his father with his kindness and loyalty.

Then the prince went again to his teacher and asked, 'How best can I serve my father and the people, here in the capital city?' The wise teacher replied, 'Ask the king to let you be the one to collect fees and taxes, and distribute benefits to the people. If he agrees, then carry out your duties honestly and fairly, with energy and kindness.'

Again the prince followed his teacher's advice. Trusting his one-hundredth son, the king was glad to assign these functions to him. When he went out to perform the difficult task of collecting fees and taxes, the young prince was always gentle, fair and lawful. When he distributed food to the hungry, and other necessary things to the needy, he was always generous, kind and sympathetic. Before long, the one-hundredth prince gained the respect and affection of all.

Eventually, the king came to be on his deathbed. His ministers asked him who should be the next king. He said that all his one-hundred sons had a right to succeed him. It should be left up to the citizens.

After he died, all the citizens agreed to make the one-hundredth prince their next ruler. Because of his goodness, they crowned him King Gamani the Righteous.

When the ninety-nine older brothers heard what had happened, they thought they had been insulted. Filled with envy and rage, they prepared for war. They sent a message to King Gamani, which said, 'We are all your elders. Neighbour countries will laugh at us if we are ruled by the one-hundredth prince. Either you give up the kingdom or we will take it by war!'

After he received this message, King Gamani took it with him to his wise old teacher, and asked his advice.

It just so happened that this honorable gentle teacher was the reborn Enlightenment Being. He said, 'Tell them you refuse to wage war against your brothers. Tell them you will not help them kill innocent people you have come to know and love. Tell them that, instead, you are dividing the king's wealth among all one-hundred princes. Then send each one his portion.' Again the king obeyed his teacher.

Meanwhile the ninety-nine older princes had brought their ninety-nine small armies to surround the royal capital. When they received the king's message and their small portions of the royal treasure, they held a meeting. They decided that each portion was so small it was almost meaningless. Therefore, they would not accept them.

But then they realized that, in the same way, if they fought with King Gamani and then with each other, the kingdom itself would be divided into small worthless portions. Each small piece of the once-great kingdom would be weak in the face of any unfriendly country. So they sent back their portions of the royal treasure as offerings of peace, and accepted the rule of King Gamani.

The king was pleased, and invited his brothers to the palace to celebrate the peace and unity of the kingdom. He entertained them in the most perfect ways—with generosity, pleasant conversation, providing instruction for their benefit, and treating all with even-handed courtesy.

In this way, the king and the ninety-nine princes became closer as friends than they had been as brothers. They were strong in their support of each other. This was known in all the surrounding countries, so no one threatened the kingdom or its people. After a few months, the ninety-nine brothers returned to their provinces.

King Gamani the Righteous invited his wise old teacher to live in the palace. He honored him with great wealth and many gifts. He held a celebration for his respected teacher, saying to the full court, 'I, who was the one-hundredth prince, among one-hundred worthy princes, owe all my success to the wise advice of my generous and understanding teacher. Likewise, all who follow their wise teachers' advice will earn prosperity and happiness. Even the unity and strength of the kingdom, we owe to my beloved teacher.'

The kingdom prospered under the remainder of the generous and just rule of King Gamani the Righteous.

The moral is: One is rewarded a hundred-fold for following the advice of a wise teacher.

The King With One Grey Hair

A very, very long time ago, there were people who lived much longer than they do today. They lived many thousand years. At that time, the Enlightenment Being was born as a baby named Makhadeva. He lived 84,000 years as a child and crown prince. At the time of our story, he had been a young king for 80,000 years.

One day, Makhadeva told the royal barber, 'If you see any grey hair on my head, you must tell me immediately!' Of course, the barber promised to do so.

Another 4,000 years passed, until Makhadeva had been a young king for 84,000 years. Then one day, while he was cutting the king's hair, the royal barber saw just one little grey hair on all the king's head. So he said, 'Oh my lord, I see one grey hair on your head.' The king said, 'If this be so, pull it out and put it in my hand.' The barber got his golden tweezers, plucked out the single little grey hair, and put it in the king's hand.

At that time, the king still had at least another 84,000 years left to live as an old king! Looking at the one grey hair in his hand, he became very afraid of dying. He felt like death was closing in on him, as if he were trapped in a burning house. He was so afraid, that the sweat rolled down his back, and he shuddered.

King Makhadeva thought, 'Oh foolish king, you have wasted all this long life and now you are near death. You have made no attempt to destroy your greed and envy, to live without hating, and to get rid of your ignorance by learning the truth and becoming wise.'

As he thought this, his body burned and the sweat kept rolling down. Then he decided once and for all, 'It is time to give up the kingship, be ordained as a monk, and practice meditation!' Thinking so, he granted the income of a whole town to the barber. It amounted to one-hundred-thousand per year.

Then the king called his oldest son to him and said, 'My son, I have seen a grey hair. I have become old. I have enjoyed the worldly pleasures of great wealth and power. When I die, I want to be reborn in a heaven world, to enjoy the pleasures of the gods. So I will be ordained as a monk. You must now take the responsibility of ruling the country. I will live the life of a monk in the forest.'

Hearing this, the royal ministers and the rest of the court rushed to the king and said, 'Our lord, why do you suddenly want to be ordained?'

The king held up the grey hair in his hand and said, 'My ministers and subjects, I have realized that this grey hair shows that the three stages of life—youth, middle age and old age—are coming to an end. This first grey hair was the messenger of death sitting on my head. Grey hairs are like angels sent by the god of death. Therefore, this very day is the time for me to be ordained.'

The people wept at the news of his departure. King Makhadeva gave up his royal life, went into the forest, and was ordained as a monk. There he practiced what holy men call the 'Four Heavenly States of Mind'. First is loving-kindness, tender affection for all. Second is feeling sympathy and pity for all those who suffer. Third is feeling happiness for all those who are joyful. And the fourth state is balance and calm even in the face of difficulties or troubles.

After 84,000 years of great effort meditating and practicing these states as a humble forest monk, the Bodhisatta died. He was reborn in a high heaven world, to live a life a million years long!

The moral is: Even a long life is too short to waste.

The Happy Monk

Once upon a time, there was a high class rich man. As he became older, he realised that the suffering of old age was about the same for rich and poor alike. So he gave up his wealth and class position, and went into the forest to live as a poor monk. He practiced meditation, and developed his mind. He freed himself from unwholesome thoughts, and became content and happy. His peacefulness and friendliness gradually drew 500 followers to his side.

At that time, long ago, most monks usually looked pretty serious. But there was one monk who, even though he was quite dignified, always wore at least a little smile. No matter what happened, he never lost this glimmer of inner happiness. And on happy occasions, he had the broadest smile, and the warmest laughter of all.

Sometimes monks, as well as others, would ask him why he was so happy that he always wore a smile. He chuckled and said, 'If I told you, you wouldn't believe me! And if you thought I spoke a lie, it would be a dishonour to my master.' The wise old master knew the source of the happiness that could not be wiped from his face. He made this happiest monk his number one assistant.

One year, after the rainy season, the old monk and his 500 followers went to the city. The king permitted them to live in his pleasure garden for the springtime.

This king was a good man, who took his responsibilities as ruler seriously. He tried to protect the people from danger, and to increase their prosperity and welfare. He always had to worry about neighbouring kings, some of whom were unfriendly and threatening. He often had to make peace between his own rival ministers of state.

Sometimes his wives fought for his attention, and for the advancement of their sons. Occasionally, a dissatisfied subject even threatened the life of the king himself! And, of course, he had to worry constantly about the finances of the kingdom. In fact, he had so much to worry about, that he never had time to be happy!

As summer approached, he learned that the monks were preparing to return to the forest. Considering the health and welfare of the old leader, the king went to him and said, 'Your reverence, you are now very old and weak. What good does it do to go back to the forest? You can send your followers back, while you remain here.'

The chief monk then called his number one assistant to him and said, 'You are now to be the leader of the other monks, while you all live in the forest. As I am too old and weak. I will remain here as offered by the king.' So the 500 returned to the forest and the old one remained.

The number one assistant continued practicing meditation in the forest. He gained so much wisdom and peace that he became even happier than before. He missed the master, and wanted to share his happiness with him. So he returned to the city for a visit.

When he arrived, he sat on a rug at the feet of the old monk. They didn't speak very much, but every so often the number one assistant would say, 'What happiness! Oh what happiness!'

Then the king came to visit. He paid his respects to the chief monk. However, the one from the forest just kept saying, 'What happiness! Oh what happiness!' He did not even stop to greet the king and show proper respect. This disturbed him, and he thought, 'With all my worries, as busy as I am looking after the kingdom, I take time out for a visit and this monk does not respect me enough to even recognize me. How insulting!' He said to the senior of the two monks, 'Venerable sir, this monk must be stupid from overeating. That must be why he is so full of happiness. Does he lie around here lazily all the time?'

The head monk replied, 'Oh king, have patience and I will tell you the source of his happiness. Not many know it. He was once a king, just as rich and mighty as you! Then he was ordained a monk and gave up his kingly life. Now he thinks his old happiness was nothing compared to his present joy!

'He used to be surrounded by armed men, who guarded and protected him. Now, sitting alone in the forest with nothing to fear, he has no need for armed guards. He has given up the burden of worrying about wealth that has to be protected. Instead, free of the worry of wealth and the fear of power, his wisdom protects himself and others. He advances in meditation to such inner peace, that he cannot keep from saying, 'What happiness! Oh what happiness!''

The king understood at once. Hearing the story of the happy monk made him feel at peace. He stayed for a while and received advice from both of them. Then he honoured them, and returned to the palace.

Later the happy monk, who once had been a king, paid his respects to his master and returned to the lovely forest. The old chief monk lived out the remainder of his life, died, and was reborn in a high heaven world.

The moral is: Unattached to wealth and power, happiness increases.

Beauty and Grey

Once upon a time, there was a deer who was the leader of a herd of a thousand. He had two sons. One was very slim and tall, with bright alert eyes, and smooth reddish fur. He was called Beauty. The other was grey in colour, also slim and tall, and was called Grey.

One day, after they were fully grown, their father called Beauty and Grey to him. He said, 'I am now very old, so I cannot do all that is necessary to look after this big herd of deer. I want you, my two grown-up children, to be the leaders, while I retire from looking after them all the time. We will divide the herd, and each of you will lead 500 deer.' So it was done.

In India, when the harvest time comes, the deer are always in danger. The rice is at its tallest, and the deer cannot help but go into the paddies and eat it. To avoid the destruction of their crops, the human beings dig pits, set sharp stakes in the ground, and build stone traps—all to capture and kill the deer.

Knowing this was the season, the wise old deer called the two new leaders to him. He advised them to take the herd up into the mountain forest, far from the dangerous farm lands. This was how he had always saved the deer from being wounded or killed. Then he would bring them back to the low lands after the harvest was over.

Since he was too old and weak for the trip, he would remain behind in hiding. He warned them to be careful and have a safe journey. Beauty set out with his herd for the mountain forest, and so did Grey with his.

The villagers all along the way knew that this was the time the deer moved from the low lying farm lands to the high countryside. So they hid along the way and killed the deer as they passed by.

Grey did not pay attention to his father's wise advice. Instead of being careful and travelling safely, he was in a hurry to get to the lush mountain forest. So he moved his herd constantly, during the night, at dawn and dusk, and even in broad daylight. This made it easy for the people to shoot the deer in Grey's herd with bows and arrows. Many were killed, and many were wounded, only to die in pain later on. Grey reached the forest with only a few deer remaining alive.

The tall sleek red-furred Beauty was wise enough to understand the danger to his moving herd. So he was very careful. He knew it was safer to stay away from the villages, and from all humans. He knew it was not safe in the daytime, or even at dawn or dusk. So he led his herd wide around the villages, and moved only in the middle of the night. Beauty's herd arrived in the mountain forest safe and sound, with no one killed or injured.

The two herds found each other, and remained in the mountains until well after the harvest season was over. Then they began the return to the farmland country.

Grey had learned nothing from the first trip. As it was getting cold in the mountains, he was in a hurry to get to the warmer low lands. So he was just as careless as before. Again the people hid along the way and attacked and killed the deer. All Grey's herd were killed, later to be eaten or sold by the villagers. Grey himself was the only one who survived the journey.

Beauty led his herd in the same careful way as before. He brought back all 500 deer, completely safe. While the deer were still in the distance, the old chief said to his doe, 'Look at the deer coming back to us. Beauty has all his followers with him. Grey comes limping back alone, without his whole herd of 500. Those who follow a wise leader, with good qualities, will always be safe. Those who follow a foolish leader, who is careless and thinks only of himself, will fall into troubles and be destroyed.'

After some time, the old deer died and was reborn as he deserved. Beauty became chief of the herd and lived a long life, loved and admired by all.

The moral is: A wise leader puts the safety of his followers first.

Mountain Buck and Village Doe

Once upon a time, in northern India, there was a herd of village deer. They were used to being near villages; they were born there and grew up there. They knew they had to be very careful around people. This was especially true at harvest time, when the crops were tall, and the farmers trapped and killed any deer who came near.

At harvest time, the village deer stayed in the forest all day long. They only came near the village during the dark of the night. One of these was a beautiful young doe. She had soft reddish-brown fur, a fluffy white tail and big, wide, bright eyes.

During this particular season, there was a young mountain buck who had strayed into the same low forest. One day, he saw the beautiful young doe, and immediately became infatuated with her. He didn't know anything about her. But he imagined himself to be deeply in love with her, just because of her reddish-brown fur and her fluffy white tail and her big wide bright eyes. He even dreamed about her, although she did not know he existed!

After a few days, the young mountain buck decided to introduce himself. As he was walking out into the clearing where she was grazing, he was entranced by her appearance and could not take his eyes off her. He began speaking: 'Oh my sweet beauty, as lovely as the stars and as bright as the moon, I confess to you that I am deeply—' Just then, the young buck's hoof got caught in a root, he tripped and fell, and his face splashed in a mud puddle! The pretty village doe was flattered, so she smiled. But inside, she thought this mountain buck was really rather silly!

Meanwhile, unknown to the deer, there was a clan of tree fairies living in that part of the forest. They had been watching the mountain buck, while he secretly watched the village doe. When he walked out into the clearing, began his speech, and fell in the mud puddle, the fairies laughed and laughed. 'What fools these dumb animals are!' they cried. But one fairy did not laugh. He said,'I fear this is a warning of danger to this young fool!'

The young buck was a little embarrassed, but he did not see it as any kind of warning. From then on, he followed the doe wherever she went. He kept telling her how beautiful she was and how much he loved her. She didn't pay much attention.

Then night came, and it was time for the doe to go down to the village. The people who lived along the way knew the deer passed by at night. So they set traps to catch them. That night a hunter waited, hiding behind a bush.

Carefully, the village doe set out. The mountain buck, who was still singing her praises, went right along with her. She stopped and said to him, 'My dear buck, you are not experienced with being around villages. You don't know how dangerous human beings are. The village, and the way to it, can bring death to a deer even at night. Since you are so young and inexperienced (and she thought to herself, 'and foolish'), you should not come down to the village with me. You should remain in the safety of the forest.'

At this, the tree fairies applauded. But of course, the deer could not hear them.

The young buck paid no attention to the doe's warning. He just said, 'Your eyes look so lovely in the moonlight!' and kept walking with her. She said, 'If you won't listen to me, at least be quiet!' He was so infatuated with her, that he could not control his mind. But he did finally shut his mouth!

After a while, they approached the place where the hunter was hiding behind a bush. The fairies saw him, and became agitated and frightened for the deer's safety. They flew nervously around the tree, branches, but they could only watch.

The doe could smell the hiding man. She was afraid of a trap. So, thinking to save her own life, she let the buck go first. She followed a little way behind.

When the hunter saw the unsuspecting mountain buck, he shot his arrow and killed him instantly. Seeing this, the terrified doe turned tail and ran back to the forest clearing as fast as she could.

The hunter claimed his kill. He started a fire, skinned the deer, cooked some of the venison and ate his fill. Then he threw the carcass over his shoulder and carried it back home to feed his family.

When the fairies saw what happened, some of them cried. As they watched the hunter cut up the once noble-looking buck, some of them felt sick. Others blamed the careful doe for leading him to the slaughter.

But the wise fairy, who had given the first warning, said, 'It was the excitement of infatuation that killed this foolish deer. Such blind desire brings false happiness at first, but ends in pain and suffering.'

The moral is: Infatuation leads to destruction.

The Wind-deer and the Honey-grass

Once upon a time, the King of Benares had a gardener who looked after his pleasure garden. Animals sometimes came into the garden from the nearby forest. The gardener complained about this to the king, who said, 'If you see any strange animal, tell me at once.'

One day, he saw a strange kind of deer at the far end of the garden. When he saw the man, he ran like the wind. That is why they are called 'wind-deer'. They are a rare breed that are extremely timid. They are very easily frightened by human beings.

The gardener told the king about the wind-deer. He asked the gardener if he could catch the rare animal. He replied, 'My lord, if you give me some bee's honey, I could even bring him into the palace!' So the king ordered that he be given as much bee's honey as he wanted.

This particular wind-deer loved to eat the flowers and fruits in the king's pleasure garden. The gardener let himself be seen by him little by little, so he would be less frightened. Then he began to smear honey on the grass where the wind-deer usually came to eat. Sure enough, the deer began eating the honey-smeared grass. Soon he developed a craving for the taste of this 'honey-grass'. The craving made him come to the garden every day. Before long, he would eat nothing else!

Little by little, the gardener came closer and closer to the wind-deer. At first, he would run away. But later, he lost his fear and came to think the man was harmless. As the gardener became more and more friendly, eventually he got the deer to eat the honey-grass right out of his hand. He continued doing this for some time, in order to build up his confidence and trust.

Meanwhile, the gardener had rows of curtains set up, making a wide pathway from the far end of the pleasure garden to the king's palace. From inside this pathway, the curtains would keep the wind-deer from seeing any people that might scare him.

When all was prepared, the gardener took a bag of grass and a container of honey with him. Again he began hand-feeding the wind-deer when he appeared. Gradually, he led the wind-deer into the curtained-off pathway. Slowly, he continued to lead him with the honey-grass, until finally the deer followed him right into the palace. Once inside, the palace guards closed the doors, and the wind-deer was trapped. Seeing the people of the court, he suddenly became very frightened and began running around, madly trying to escape.

The king came down to the hall and saw the panic-stricken wind-deer. He said, 'What a wind-deer! How could he have gotten into such a state? A wind-deer is an animal who will not return to a place where he has so much as seen a human, for seven full days. Ordinarily, if a wind-deer is at all frightened in a particular place, he will not return for the rest of his life! But look! Even such a shy wild creature can be enslaved by his craving for the taste of something sweet. Then he can be lured into the centre of the city and even inside the palace itself.

'My friends, the teachers warn us not to be too attached to the place we live, for all things pass away. They say that being too attached to a small circle of friends is confining and restricts a broad outlook. But see how much more dangerous is the simple craving for a sweet flavour, or any other taste sensation. See how this beautiful shy animal was trapped by my gardener, by taking advantage of his craving for taste.'

Not wishing to harm the gentle wind-deer, the king had him released into the forest. He never returned to the royal pleasure garden, and he never missed the taste of honey-grass.

The moral is: It is better to eat to live, than to live to eat.

The Fawn Who Played Hookey

Once upon a time there was a herd of forest deer. In this herd was a wise and respected teacher, cunning in the ways of deer. He taught the tricks and strategies of survival to the young fawns.

One day, his younger sister brought her son to him, to be taught what is so important for deer. She said, 'Oh brother teacher, this is my son. Please teach him the tricks and strategies of deer.' The teacher said to the fawn, 'Very well, you can come at this time tomorrow for your first lesson.'

At first, the young deer came to the lessons as he was supposed to. But soon, he became more interested in playing with the other young bucks and does. He didn't realize how dangerous it could be for a deer who learned nothing but deer games. So he started cutting classes. Soon he was playing hooky all the time.

Unfortunately, one day the fawn who played hooky stepped in a snare and was trapped. Since he was missing, his mother worried. She went to her brother the teacher, and asked him, 'My dear brother, how is my son? Have you taught your nephew the tricks and strategies of deer?'

The teacher replied, 'My dear sister, your son was disobedient and unteachable. Out of respect for you, I tried my best to teach him. But he did not want to learn the tricks and strategies of deer. He played hooky! How could I possibly teach him? You are obedient and faithful, but he is not. It is useless to try to teach him.'

Later they heard the sad news. The stubborn fawn who played hooky had been trapped and killed by a hunter. He skinned him and took the meat home to his family.

The moral is: Nothing can be learned from a teacher by one who misses the class.

The Fawn Who Played Dead

Once upon a time, there was a herd of forest deer. In this herd was a wise and respected teacher, cunning in the ways of deer. He taught the tricks and strategies of survival to the young fawns.

One day, his younger sister brought her son to him, to be taught what is so important for deer. She said, 'Oh brother teacher, this is my son. Please teach him the tricks and strategies of deer.' The teacher said to the fawn, 'Very well, you can come at this time tomorrow for your first lesson.'

The young deer came to the lessons as he was supposed to. When others cut classes to spend all day playing, he remained and paid attention to the good teacher. He was well-liked by the other young bucks and does, but he only played when his class work was complete. Being curious to learn, he was always on time for the lessons. He was also patient with the other students, knowing that some learn more quickly than others. He respected the teacher deer for his knowledge, and was grateful for his willingness to share it.

One day, the fawn stepped in a trap in the forest and was captured. He cried out in great pain. This frightened the other fawns, who ran back to the herd and told his mother. She was terrified, and ran to her brother the teacher. Trembling with fear, crying big tears, she said to him, 'Oh my dear brother, have you heard the news that my son has been trapped by a hunter's snare? How can I save my little child's life? Did he study well in your presence?'

Her brother said, 'My sister, don't be afraid. I have no doubt he will be safe. He studied hard and always did his very best. He never missed a class and always paid attention. Therefore, there is no need to have doubt or pain in your heart. He will not be hurt by any human being. Don't worry. I am confident he will return to you and make you happy again. He has learned all the tricks and strategies used by deer to cheat the hunters. So be patient. He will return!'

Meanwhile, the trapped fawn was thinking, 'All my friends were afraid and ran away. There is no one to help me get out of this deadly trap. Now I must use the tricks and strategies I learned from the wise teacher who taught so well.'

The deer strategy he decided to use was the one called, 'playing dead.' First, he used his hoofs to dig up the dirt and grass, to make it look like he had tried very hard to escape. Then he relieved his bowels and released his urine, because this is what happens when a deer is caught in a trap and dies in very great fear. Next, he covered his body with his own saliva.

Lying stretched out on his side, he held his body rigidly and stiffened his legs out straight. He turned up his eyes, and let his tongue hang out of the side of his mouth. He filled his lungs with air and puffed out his belly. Finally, with his head leaning on one side, he breathed through the nostril next to the ground, not through the upper one.

Lying motionless, he looked so much like a stiff corpse that flies flew around him, attracted by the awful smells. Crows stood nearby waiting to eat his flesh.

Before long it was early morning and the hunter came to inspect his traps. Finding the fawn who was playing dead, he slapped the puffed up belly and found it stiff. Seeing the flies and the mess he thought, 'Ah, it has already started to stiffen. He must have been trapped much earlier this morning. No doubt the tender meat is already starting to spoil. I will skin and butcher the carcass right here, and carry the meat home.'

Since he completely believed the deer was dead, he removed and cleaned the trap, and began spreading leaves to make a place to do the butchering. Realizing he was free, the fawn suddenly sprang to his feet. He ran like a little cloud blown by a swift wind, back to the comfort and safety of his mother. The whole herd celebrated his survival, thanks to learning so well from the wise teacher.

The moral is: Well-learned lessons bring great rewards.

The Wind and the Moon

Once upon a time, there were two very good friends who lived together in the shade of a rock. Strange as it may seem, one was a lion and one was a tiger. They had met when they were too young to know the difference between lions and tigers. So they did not think their friendship was at all unusual. Besides, it was a peaceful part of the mountains, possibly due to the influence of a gentle forest monk who lived nearby. He was a hermit, one who lives far away from other people.

For some unknown reason, one day the two friends got into a silly argument. The tiger said, 'Everyone knows the cold comes when the moon wanes from full to new!' The lion said, 'Where did you hear such nonsense? Everyone knows the cold comes when the moon waxes from new to full!'

The argument got stronger and stronger. Neither could convince the other. They could not reach any conclusion to resolve the growing dispute. They even started calling each other names! Fearing for their friendship, they decided to go ask the learned forest monk, who would surely know about such things.

Visiting the peaceful hermit, the lion and tiger bowed respectfully and put their question to him. The friendly monk thought for a while and then gave his answer. 'It can be cold in any phase of the moon, from new to full and back to new again. It is the wind that brings the cold, whether from west or north or east. Therefore, in a way, you are both right! And neither of you is defeated by the other. The most important thing is to live without conflict, to remain united. Unity is best by all means.'

The lion and tiger thanked the wise hermit. They were happy to still be friends.

The moral is: Weather comes and weather goes, but friendship remains.

The Goat Who Saved the Priest

Once upon a time, there was a very famous priest in a very old religion. He decided it was the right day to perform the ritual sacrificing of a goat. In his ignorance, he thought this as an offering demanded by his god.

He obtained an appropriate goat for the sacrifice. He ordered his servants to take the goat to the holy river and wash him and decorate him with flower garlands. Then they were to wash themselves, as part of the purification practice.

Down at the riverbank, the goat suddenly understood that today he would definitely be killed. He also became aware of his past births and deaths and rebirths. He realized that the results of his past unwholesome deeds were about to finally be completed. So he laughed an uproarious goat-laugh, like the clanging of cymbals.

In the midst of his laughter, he realized another truth—that the priest, by sacrificing him, would suffer the same terrible results, due to his ignorance. So he began to cry as loudly as he had just been laughing!

The servants, who were bathing in the holy river, heard first the laughing and then the crying. They were amazed. So they asked the goat, 'Why did you loudly laugh and then just as loudly cry? What is the reason for this?' He replied, 'I will tell you the reason. But it must be in the presence of your master, the priest.'

Since they were very curious, they immediately took

the sacrificial goat to the priest. They explained all that had happened. The priest, too, became very curious. He respectfully asked the goat, 'Sir, why did you laugh so loudly, and then just as loudly cry?'

The goat, remembering his past lives, said, 'A long time ago, I, too, was a priest who, like you, was well educated in the sacred religious rites. I thought that to sacrifice a goat was a necessary offering to my god, which would benefit others, as well as myself in future rebirths. However, the true result of my actions was that in my next 499 lives I myself have been beheaded!

'While being prepared for the sacrifice, I realized that today I will definitely lose my head for the 500th time. Then I will finally be free of all the results of my unwholesome deeds of so long ago. The joy of this made me laugh uncontrollably.

'Then I suddenly realized that you, the priest, were about to repeat the same unwholesome action, and would be doomed to the same result of having your head chopped off in your next 500 lives! So, out of compassion and sympathy, my laughter turned to tears.'

The priest was afraid this goat might be right, so he said, 'Well, sir goat, I will not kill you.' The goat replied, 'Reverend priest, even if you do not kill me, I know that today I will lose my head and finally be released from the results of my past unwholesome action.'

The priest said, 'Don't be afraid, my fine goat. I will provide the very best protection and personally guarantee that no harm will come to you.' But the goat said, 'Oh priest, your protection is very weak, compared to the power of my unwholesome deed to cause its necessary results.'

So the priest cancelled the sacrifice, and began to have doubts about killing innocent animals. He released the goat and, along with his servants, followed him in order to protect him from any danger.

The goat wandered into a rocky place. He saw some tender leaves on a branch and stretched out his neck to reach them. All of a sudden a thunderstorm appeared out of nowhere. A lightning bolt struck an over-hanging rock, and cut off a sharp slab, which fell and chopped off the goat's head! He died instantly, and the thunderstorm disappeared.

Hearing of this very strange event, hundreds of local people came to the place. No one could understand how it had happened.

There was also a fairy who lived in a nearby tree. He had seen all that had occurred. He appeared, gently fluttering in the air overhead. He began to teach the curious people, saying, 'Look at what happened to this poor goat. This was the result of killing animals! All beings are born, and suffer through sickness, old age and death. But all wish to live, and not to die. Not seeing that all have this in common, some kill other living beings. This causes suffering also to those who kill, both now and in countless future rebirths.

'Being ignorant that all deeds must cause results to the doer, some continue to kill and heap up more suffering on themselves in the future. Each time they kill, a part of themselves must also die in this present life. And the suffering continues even by rebirth in hell worlds!' Those who heard the fairy speak felt that they were very lucky indeed. They gave up their ignorant killing, and were far better off, both in this life, and in pleasant rebirths.

The moral is: Even religion can be a source of ignorance.

The God in the Banyan Tree

In the past, and even in some places today, people have had superstitions. One such is that a large or unusual tree is inhabited by a tree god, or some kind of spirit. People think that they can make a promise to this tree god, so he will help them in some way. When they think the god has helped them, then they must keep their promise.

Once upon a time, in the city of Kasi in northern India, a man came upon a large banyan tree. He immediately thought there must be a god living there. So he made a promise to this tree god that he would perform an animal sacrifice, in return for a wish being granted.

It just so happened that his wish was fulfilled, but whether by a god or a demon or by some other means, no one knows. The man was sure the tree god had answered his prayer, so he wanted to keep his promise.

Since it was a big wish, it called for a big sacrifice. He brought many goats, mules, chickens and sheep. He collected firewood and prepared to burn the helpless animals as a sacrifice.

The spirit living in the banyan tree appeared and said, 'Oh friend, you made a promise. You are now bound by that promise. You think you must keep the promise in order to be released from the bondage to it. But if you commit such terrible unwholesome acts, even though promised, the unpleasant results will put you in much greater bondage. For you will be forced to suffer those results in this life, and even by rebirths in hell! The way to release yourself into future deliverance is to give up unwholesome actions, no matter what!

'And furthermore, since you think I'm a true god, what makes you think I eat meat? Haven't you heard that we gods eat better things, like 'ambrosia' or stardust or sunbeams? I have no need of meat or any other food offerings.' Then he disappeared.

The foolish man understood the mistake he had made. Instead of doing unwholesome deeds that would force unhappy results on him in the future, he began to do only wholesome deeds that would benefit himself and others.

The moral is: Keeping a bad promise is worse than making it.

The Monkey King and the Water Demon

Once upon a time, far away in a deep forest, there was a nation of 80,000 monkeys. They had a king who was unusually large, as big as a fawn. He was not only big in body, he was also 'large in mind'. After all, he was the Bodhisatta—the Enlightenment Being.

One day, he advised his monkey nation by saying, 'My subjects, there are poisonous fruits in this deep forest, and ponds possessed by demons. So if you see any unusual fruit or unknown pond, do not eat or drink until you ask me first.' Paying close attention to their wise king, all the monkeys agreed to follow his advice.

Later on, they came to an unknown pond. Even though they were all tired and thirsty from searching for food, no one would drink without first asking the monkey king. So they sat in the trees and on the ground around the pond.

When he arrived, the monkey king asked them, 'Did anyone drink the water?' They replied, 'No, your majesty, we followed your instructions.' He said, 'Well done.'

Then he walked along the bank, around the pond. He examined the footprints of the animals that had gone into the water, and saw that none came out again! So he realized this pond must be possessed by a water demon. He said to the 80,000 monkeys, 'This pond is possessed by a water demon. Do not anybody go into it.'

After a little while, the water demon saw that none of the monkeys went into the water to drink. So he rose out of the middle of the pond, taking the shape of a frightening monster. He had a big blue belly, a white face with bulging green eyes, and red claws and feet. He said, 'Why are you just sitting around? Come into the pond and drink at once!'

The monkey king said to the horrible monster, 'Are you the water demon who owns this pond?' 'Yes, I am,' said he. 'Do you eat whoever goes into the water?' asked the king. 'Yes, I do,' he answered, 'including even birds. I eat them all. And when you are forced by your thirst to come into the pond and drink, I will enjoy eating you, the biggest monkey, most of all!' He grinned, and saliva dripped down his hairy chin.

But the monkey king with the well-trained mind remained calm. He said, 'I will not let you eat me or a single one of my followers. And yet, we will drink all the water we want!' The water demon grunted, 'Impossible! How will you do that?' The monkey king replied, 'Each one of the 80,000 of us will drink using bamboo shoots as straws. And you will not be able to touch us!'

Of course, anyone who has seen bamboo knows there is a difficulty. Bamboo grows in sections, one after another, with a knot between each one. Any one section is too small, so the demon could grab the monkey, pull him under and gobble him up. But the knots make it impossible to sip through more than one section.

The monkey king was very special, and that is why so many followed him. In the past, he had practiced goodness and trained his mind with such effort and attention, that he had developed very fine qualities of mind. This is why he was said to be 'large in mind', not because he simply had a 'big brain'.

The Enlightenment Being was able to keep these fine qualities in his mind, and produce a very unlikely event—a miracle. First, he took a young bamboo shoot, blew through it to make the knots disappear, and used it to sip water from the pond. Then, amazing as it may sound, he waved his hand and all the bamboo growing around that one pond lost their knots. They became a new kind of bamboo.

Then, all his 80,000 followers picked bamboo shoots and easily drank their fill from the pond. The water demon could not believe his green eyes. Grumbling to himself, he slid back under the surface, leaving only gurgling bubbles behind.

The moral is: Test the water before jumping in.

The Tree That Acted Like a Hunter

Once upon a time, there was an antelope who lived in the deep forest. He ate the fruits that fell from the trees. There was one tree that had become his favorite.

In the same area there was a hunter who captured and killed antelopes and deer. He put down fruit as bait under a tree. Then he waited, hiding in the branches above. He held a rope noose hanging down to the ground around the fruits. When an animal ate the fruit, the hunter tightened the noose and caught him.

Early one morning the antelope came to his favorite tree in search of fruits to eat. He did not see that the hunter was hiding in it, with his noose-trap ready. Even though he was hungry, the antelope was very careful. He was on the lookout for any possible danger. He saw the delicious looking ripe fruits at the foot of his favourite tree. He wondered why no animal had yet eaten any, and so he was afraid something was wrong.

The hiding hunter saw the antelope approaching from a distance. Seeing him stop and take great care, he was afraid he would not be able to trap him. He was so anxious that he began throwing fruits in the direction of the antelope, trying to lure him into coming closer.

But this was a pretty smart antelope. He knew that fruits only fall straight down when they fall from trees. Since these fruits were flying towards him, he knew there was danger. So he examined the tree itself very carefully, and saw the hunter in the branches. However, he pretended not to see him.

He spoke in the direction of the tree. 'Oh my dear fruit tree, you used to give me your fruits by letting them fall straight down to the ground. Now, throwing them towards me, you do not act at all like a tree! Since you have changed your habits, I too will change mine. I will get my fruits from a different tree from now on, one that still acts like a tree!'

The hunter realized his mistake and saw that the antelope had outsmarted him. This angered him and he yelled out, 'You may escape me this time, you clever antelope, but I'll get you next time for sure!'

The antelope realized that by getting so angry, the hunter had given himself away a second time. So he spoke in the direction of the tree again. 'Not only don't you act like a tree, but you act like a hunter! You foolish humans, who live by killing animals. You do not understand that killing the innocent brings harm also to you, both in this life and by rebirth in a hell world. It is clear that we antelopes are far wiser than you. We eat fruits, we remain innocent of killing others, and we avoid the harmful results.'

So saying, the careful antelope leaped into the thick forest and was gone.

The moral is: The wise remain innocent.

The Dog King Silver

Once upon a time the King of Benares went to his pleasure garden in his fancy decorated chariot. He loved this chariot, mostly because of the rich hand-worked leather belts and straps.

On this occasion, he stayed in his pleasure garden all day long and into the evening. It was late when he finally got back to the palace. So the chariot was left outside in the compound all night, instead of being locked up properly.

During the night it rained heavily, and the leather got wet, swelled up, became soft, and gave off an odour. The pampered palace dogs smelled the delicious leather scent and came down into the compound. They chewed off and devoured the soft wet chariot straps. Before daybreak, they returned unseen to their places in the palace.

When the king woke up and came down, he saw that the leather had been chewed off and eaten by dogs. He called the servants and demanded to know how this happened.

Since they were supposed to watch the palace dogs, the servants were afraid to blame them. Instead, they made up a story that stray dogs, the mutts and mongrels of the city, had come into the grounds through sewers and storm drains. They were the ones who had eaten the fancy leather.

The king flew into a terrible rage. He was so overcome by anger that he decided to take vengeance against all dogs. So he decreed that whenever anyone in the city saw a dog, he was to kill him or her at once!

The people began killing dogs. The dogs could not understand why suddenly they were being killed. Later that day, they learned of the king's decree. They became very frightened and retreated to the cemetery just outside the city. This was where their leader lived, the dog king Silver.

Silver was king not because he was the biggest or strongest or toughest. He was average in size, with sleek silver fur, sparkling black eyes and alert pointed ears. He walked with great dignity, that brought admiration and respect from men as well as dogs. In his long life he had learned much, and was able to concentrate his mind on what is most important. So he became the wisest of all the dogs, as well as the one who cared most for the others. Those were the reasons he was king of the dogs.

In the cemetery, the dogs were in a panic. They were frightened to death. The dog king Silver asked them why this was. They told him all about the chariot straps and the king's decree, and the people killing them whenever they saw them.

King Silver knew there was no way to get into the well-guarded palace grounds. So he understood that the leather must have been eaten by the dogs living inside the palace.

He thought, 'We dogs know that no matter how different we may appear, somehow we are all related. So now I must make my greatest effort to save the lives of all these poor dogs, my relatives. There is no one to save them but me.'

He comforted them by saying, 'Do not be afraid. I will save you all. Stay here in the cemetery and don't go into the city. I will tell the King of Benares who are the thieves and who are the innocent. The truth will save us all.'

Before setting out, he went to a different part of the cemetery to be alone. Having practiced goodness all his life, and trained his mind, he now concentrated very hard and filled his mind with feelings of loving-kindness. He thought, 'May all dogs be well and happy, and may all dogs be safe. I go to the palace for the sake of dogs and men alike. No one shall attack or harm me.'

Then the dog king Silver began walking slowly through the streets of Benares. Because his mind was focused, he had no fear. Because of his long life of goodness, he walked with a calm dignity that demanded respect. And because of the warm glow of loving-kindness that all the people sensed, no one felt the rising of anger or any intention to harm him. Instead, they marvelled as the Great Being passed, and wondered how it could be so!

It was as if the whole city were entranced. With no obstruction, the dog king Silver walked right past the palace guards, into the royal hall of justice, and sat down calmly underneath the king's throne itself! The King of Benares was impressed by such courage and dignity. So when servants came to remove the dog, he ordered them to let him remain.

Then the dog king Silver came out from under the throne and faced the mighty King of Benares. He bowed respectfully and asked, 'Your majesty, was it you who ordered that all the dogs of the city should be killed?' 'It was I,' replied the king. 'What crime did the dogs commit?' asked the dog king. 'Dogs ate my rich beautiful chariot leather and straps.' 'Do you know which dogs did this?' asked King Silver. 'No one knows,' said the King of Benares.

'My lord,' said the dog, 'for a king such as you, who wishes to be righteous, is it right to have all dogs killed in the place of the few guilty ones? Does this do justice to the innocent ones?' The king replied, as if it made perfect sense to him, 'Since I do not know which dogs destroyed my leather, only by ordering the killing of all dogs can I be sure of punishing the guilty. The king must have justice!'

The dog king Silver paused for a moment, before challenging the king with the crucial question, 'My lord king, is it a fact that you have ordered all dogs to be killed, or are there some who are not to be killed?' The king suddenly became a little uneasy as he was forced to admit, before his whole court, 'It is true that most dogs are to be killed, but not all. The fine pure-breeds of my palace are to be spared.'

Then the dog king said, 'My lord, before you said that all dogs were to be killed, in order to ensure that the guilty would be punished. Now you say that your own palace dogs are to be spared. This shows that you have gone wrong in the way of prejudice. For a king who wishes to be righteous, it is wrong to favour some over others. The king's justice must be unbiased, like an honest scale. Although you have decreed an impartial death to all dogs, in fact this is only the slaughter of poor dogs. Your rich palace dogs are unjustly saved, while the poor are wrongly killed!'

Recognizing the truth of the dog king's words, the King of Benares asked, 'Are you wise enough to know which dogs ate my leather straps and belts?' 'Yes my lord, I do know,' said he, 'it could only be your own favourite palace dogs, and I can prove it.' 'Do so,' said the king.

The dog king asked to have the palace pets brought into the hall of justice. He asked for a mixture of buttermilk and grass, and for the dogs to be made to eat it. Lo and behold, when this was done they vomited up partly digested pieces of the king's leather straps!

Then the dog king Silver said, 'My lord, no poor dogs from the city can enter the well-guarded palace compound. You were blinded by prejudice. It is your dogs who are the guilty ones. Nevertheless, to kill any living being is an unwholesome thing to do. This is because of what we dogs know, but men do not seem to know—that somehow all life is related, so all living beings deserve the same respect as relatives.'

The whole court was amazed by what had just taken place. The King of Benares was suddenly overcome by a rare feeling of humility. He bowed before the dog king and said, 'Oh great king of dogs, I have never seen anyone such as you, one who combines perfect wisdom with great compassion. Truly, your justice is supreme. I offer my throne and the kingdom of Benares to you!'

The Enlightenment Being replied, 'Arise my lord, I have no desire for a human crown. If you wish to show your respect for me, you should be a just and merciful ruler. It would help if you begin to purify your mind by practising the 'Five Training Steps'. These are to give up entirely the five unwholesome actions: destroying life, taking what is not given, sexual wrong-doing, speaking falsely, and drunkenness.'

The king followed the teachings of the wise dog king. He ruled with great respect for all living beings. He ordered that whenever he ate, all dogs, those of the palace and those of the city, were to be fed as well. This was the beginning of the faithfulness between dogs and men that has lasted to this day.

The moral is: Prejudice leads to injustice, wisdom leads to justice.

The Great Horse Knowing-one

Once upon a time, King Brahmadatta ruled in Benares, in northern India. He had a mighty horse who had been born in the land of Sindh, in the Indus River valley of western India. Indeed, this horse was the Enlightenment Being.

As well as being big and strong, he was very intelligent and wise. When he was still young, people noticed that he always seemed to know what his rider wanted before being told. So he was called Knowing-one.

He was considered the greatest of the royal horses, and was given the very best of everything. His stall was decorated and was always kept clean and beautiful. Horses are usually faithful to their masters. Knowing-one was especially loyal, and was grateful for how well the king cared for him. Of all the royal horses, Knowing-one was also the bravest. So the king respected and trusted him.

It came to pass that seven neighbouring kings joined together to make war on King Brahmadatta. Each king brought four great armies—an elephant cavalry, a horse cavalry, a chariot brigade and ranks of foot soldiers. Together the seven kings, with all their armies, surrounded the city of Benares.

King Brahmadatta assembled his ministers and advisers to make plans for defending the kingdom. They advised him, 'Do not surrender. We must fight to protect our high positions. But you should not risk your royal person in the beginning. Instead, send out the champion of all the knights to represent you on the battlefield. If he fails, only then must you yourself go.'

So the king called the champion to him and asked, 'Can you be victorious over these seven kings?' The knight replied, 'If you permit me to ride out on the bravest and wisest, the great horse Knowing-one, only then can I win the battle.' The king agreed and said, 'My champion, it is up to you and Knowing-one to save the country in its time of danger. Take with you whatever you need.'

The champion knight went to the royal stables. He ordered that Knowing-one be well fed and dressed in protective armour, with all the finest trimmings. Then he bowed respectfully and climbed into the beautiful saddle.

Knowing-one knew the situation. He thought, 'These seven kings have come to attack my country and my king, who feeds and cares for and trusts me. Not only the seven kings, but also their large and powerful armies threaten my king and all in Benares. I cannot let them win. But I also cannot permit the champion knight to kill those kings. Then I, too, would share in the unwholesome action of taking the lives of others, in order to win an ordinary victory. Instead, I will teach a new way. I will capture all seven kings without killing anyone. That would be a truly great victory!'

Then the Knowing-one spoke to his rider. 'Sir knight, let us win this battle in a new way, without destroying life. You must only capture each king, one at a time, and remain firmly on my back. Let me find the true course through the many armies. Watch me as you ride, and I will show you the courage that goes beyond the old way, the killing way!'

As he spoke of 'a new way', and 'the true course', and 'the courage that goes beyond', it seemed the noble steed became larger than life. He reared up majestically on his powerful hind legs, and looked down on all the armies surrounding the city. The eyes of all were drawn to this magnificent one. The earth trembled as his front hoofs returned to the ground and he charged into the midst of the four armies of the first king. He seemed to have the speed of lightning, the might of a hundred elephants, and the glorious confidence of one from some other world.

The elephants could remember no such horse as this, and so the elephant cavalry retreated in fear. The horses knew that this their relative was the worthy master of them all, and so the horse cavalry and the chariot brigade stood still and bowed as the Great Being passed. And the ranks of foot-soldiers scattered like flies before a strong wind.

The first king hardly knew what had happened, before he was easily captured and brought back into the city of Benares. And so too with the second, third, fourth and fifth kings.

In the same way the sixth king was captured. But one of his loyal bodyguards leaped out from hiding and thrust his sword deep into the side of the brave Knowing-one. With blood streaming from the wound, he carried the champion knight and the captured sixth king back to the city.

When the knight saw the terrible wound, he suddenly became afraid to ride the weakened Knowing-one against the seventh king. So he began to dress in armour another powerful war horse, who was really just as big as Knowing-one.

Seeing this, though suffering in great pain from his deadly wound, Knowing-one thought, 'This champion knight has lost his courage so quickly. He has not understood the true nature of my power—the knowledge that true peace is only won by peaceful means. He tries to defeat the seventh king and his armies in the ordinary way, riding an ordinary horse.

'After taking the first step of giving up the killing of living beings, I cannot stop part way. My great effort to teach a new way would disappear like a line drawn in water!'

The great horse Knowing-one spoke to the champion knight. 'Sir knight, the seventh king and his armies are the mightiest of all. Riding an ordinary horse, even if you slaughter a thousand men and animals, you will be defeated. I, of the mighty tribe of Sindh horses, the one called Knowing-one, only I can pass through them harming none, and bring back the seventh king alive!'

The champion knight regained his courage. The brave horse struggled to his feet in great pain. While the blood continued to flow, he reared and charged through the four armies, and the knight brought back the last of the seven warlike kings. Again all those in his path were spared from harm. Seeing their seven kings in captivity, all the armies laid down their weapons and asked for peace.

Realizing that the great horse Knowing-one would not live through the night, King Brahmadatta went to see him. He had raised him from a colt, so he loved him. When he saw that he was dying, his eyes filled with tears.

Knowing-one said, 'My lord king, I have served you well. And I have gone beyond and shown a new way. Now you must grant my last request. You must not kill these seven kings, even though they have wronged you. For a bloody victory sows the seeds of the next war. Forgive their attack on you, let them return to their kingdoms, and may you all live in peace from now on.

'Whatever reward you would give to me, give instead to the champion knight. Do only wholesome deeds, be generous, honour the truth, and kill no living being. Rule with justice and compassion.'

Then he closed his eyes and breathed his last. The king burst into tears, and all mourned his passing. With the highest honours, they burned the body of the great horse Knowing-one—the Enlightenment Being.

King Brahmadatta had the seven kings brought before him. They too honoured the great one who had defeated their vast armies without spilling a drop of blood, except his own. In his memory they made peace, and never again did these seven kings and Brahmadatta make war on each other.

The moral is: True peace is only won by peaceful means.

Dirty Bathwater

Once upon a time in a kingdom in India, the finest of the royal horses was taken down to the river to be bathed. The grooms took him to the same shallow pool where they always washed him.

However, just before they arrived, a filthy dirty horse had been washed in the same spot. He had been caught in the countryside and had never had a good bath in all his life.

The fine royal horse sniffed the air. He knew right away that some filthy wild horse had bathed there and fouled the water. So he was disgusted and refused to be washed at that place.

The grooms tried their best to get him into the water, but could do nothing with him. So they went to the king and complained that the fine well-trained royal stallion had suddenly become stubborn and unmanageable.

It just so happened that the king had an intelligent minister who was known for his understanding of animals. So he called for him and said, 'Please go and see what has happened to my number one horse. Find out if he is sick or what is the reason he refuses to be bathed. Of all my horses, I thought this one was of such high quality that he would never let himself sink into dirtiness. There must be something wrong.'

The minister went down to the riverside bathing pool immediately. He found that the stately horse was not sick, but in perfect health. He noticed also that he was deliberately breathing as little as possible. So he sniffed the air and smelled a slight foul odour. Investigating further, he found that it came from the unclean water in the bathing pool. So he figured out that another very dirty horse must have been washed there, and that the king's horse was too fond of cleanliness to bathe in dirty water.

The minister asked the horse grooms, 'Has any other horse been bathed at this spot today?' 'Yes,' they replied, 'before we arrived, a dirty wild horse was bathed here.' The minister told them, 'My dear grooms, this is a fine royal horse who loves cleanliness. He does not wish to bathe in dirty water. So the thing to do is to take him up river, where the water is fresh and clean, and wash him there.'

They followed his instructions, and the royal horse was pleased to bathe in the new place.

The minister returned to the king and told what had happened. Then he said, 'You were correct your majesty, this fine horse was indeed of such high quality that he would not let himself sink into dirtiness!'

The king was amazed that his minister seemed to be able to read the mind of a horse. So he rewarded him appropriately.

The moral is: Even animals value cleanliness.

Ladyface

Once upon time, the King of Benares had a royal bull elephant who was kind, patient and harmless. Along with his sweet disposition, he had a lovely gentle face. So he was affectionately known as 'Ladyface'.

One night, a gang of robbers met together just outside the elephant shed. In the darkness they talked about their plans for robbing people. They spoke of beating and killing, and bragged that they had given up ordinary goodness so they would have no pity on their victims. They used rough he-man type gutter language, intended to scare people and show how tough they were.

Since the nights were quiet, Ladyface had nothing else to do but listen to all these terrible plans and violent rough talk. He listened carefully and, as elephants do, remembered it all. Having been brought up to obey and respect human beings, he thought these men were also to be obeyed and respected, even as teachers.

After this went on for several nights, Ladyface decided that the correct thing to do was to become rough and cruel. This usually happens to one who associates with those of a low-minded cruel nature. It happens especially to a gentle one who wishes to please others.

A 'mahout' is what the Indians call the special trainer and caretaker of a particular elephant. They are usually very close.

Early one morning, Ladyface's mahout came to see him as usual. The elephant, his mind filled with the night's robber-talk, suddenly attacked his mahout. He picked him up in his trunk, squeezed the breath out of him, and smashed him to the ground, killing him instantly. Then he picked up two other attendants, one after another, and killed them just as ferociously.

Word spread quickly through the city that the once adored Ladyface had suddenly gone mad and become a frightening man-killer. The people ran to the king for help.

It just so happened that the king had an intelligent minister who was known for his understanding of animals. So he called for him and asked him to go and determine what sickness or other condition had caused his favourite elephant to become so insanely violent.

This minister was the Bodhisatta, the Enlightenment Being. Arriving at the elephant shed, he spoke gentle soothing words to Ladyface, and calmed him down. He examined him and found him in perfect physical health. As he spoke kindly to Ladyface, he noticed that the elephant perked up his ears and paid very close attention. It was almost as if the poor animal were starved for the sound of gentle words. So the understanding minister figured out that the elephant must have been hearing the violent words or seeing the violent actions of those he mistook for teachers.

He asked the elephant guards, 'Have you seen anyone hanging around this elephant shed, at night or any other time?' 'Yes, minister,' they replied, 'for the last couple of weeks a gang of robbers has been meeting here. We were afraid to do anything, since they were such mean rough characters. Ladyface could hear their every word.'

The minister returned immediately to the king. He said, 'My lord king, your favourite elephant, Ladyface, is in perfect physical health. I have discovered that it was by hearing the rough and vulgar talk of thieves during many nights, that he has learned to be violent and cruel. Unwholesome associations often lead to unwholesome thoughts and actions.'

The king asked, 'What is to be done?' The minister said, 'Well my lord, now we must reverse the process. We must send wise men and monks, who have a high-minded kind nature, to spend just as many nights outside the elephant shed. There they should talk of the value of ordinary goodness and patience, leading to compassion, loving-kindness and harmlessness.'

So it was carried out. For several nights the kind wise ones spoke of those wonderful qualities. They used only gentle and refined language, intended to bring peacefulness and comfort to others.

Lo and behold, hearing this pleasant conversation for several nights, Ladyface the bull elephant became even more peaceful and pleasant than before!

Seeing this total change, the minister reported it to the king, saying, 'My lord, Ladyface is now even more harmless and sweet than before. Now he is as gentle as a lamb!'

The king said, 'It is wonderful indeed that such a madly violent elephant can be changed by associating with wise men and monks.' He was amazed that his minister seemed to be able to read the mind of an elephant. So he rewarded him appropriately.

The moral is: As rough talk infects with violence, so do gentle words heal with harmlessness.

Best Friends

Before the time of this story, people in Asia used to say that there would never be a time when an elephant and a dog would be friends. Elephants simply did not like dogs, and dogs were afraid of elephants.

When dogs are frightened by those who are bigger than they are, they often bark very loudly, to cover up their fear. When dogs used to do this when they saw elephants, the elephants would get annoyed and chase them. Elephants had no patience at all when it came to dogs. Even if a dog were quiet and still, any nearby elephant would automatically attack him. This is why everybody agreed that elephants and dogs were 'natural enemies', just like lions and tigers, or cats and mice.

Once upon a time there was a royal bull elephant who was very well fed and cared for. In the neighbourhood of the elephant shed, there was a scrawny, poorly fed, stray dog. He was attracted by the smell of the rich sweet rice being fed to the royal elephant. So he began sneaking into the shed and eating the wonderful rice that fell from the elephant's mouth. He liked it so much, that soon he would eat nowhere else. While enjoying his food, the big mighty elephant did not notice the tiny shy stray dog.

By eating such rich food, the once underfed dog gradually got bigger and stronger, and became very handsome looking. The good-natured elephant began to notice him. Since the dog had gotten used to being around the elephant, he had lost his fear. So he did not bark at him. Because he was not annoyed by the friendly dog, the elephant gradually got used to him.

Slowly they became friendlier and friendlier with each other. Before long, neither would eat without the other, and they enjoyed spending their time together. When they played, the dog would grab the elephant's heavy trunk, and the elephant would swing him forward and backward, from side to side, up and down, and even in circles! So it was that they became 'best friends', and wanted never to be separated.

Then one day a man from a remote village, who was visiting the city, passed by the elephant shed. He saw the frisky dog, who had become strong and beautiful. He bought him from the mahout, even though he didn't really own him. He took him back to his home village, without anyone knowing where that was.

Of course, the royal bull elephant became very sad, since he missed his best friend the dog. He became so sad that he didn't want to do anything, not even eat or drink or bathe. So the mahout had to report this to the king, although he said nothing about selling the friendly dog.

It just so happened that the king had an intelligent minister who was known for his understanding of animals. So he told him to go and find out the reason for the elephant's condition.

The wise minister went to the elephant shed. He saw at once that the royal bull elephant was very sad. He thought, 'This once happy elephant does not appear to be sick in any way. But I have seen this condition before, in men and animals alike. This elephant is grief-stricken, probably due to the loss of a very dear friend.'

Then he said to the guards and attendants, 'I find no sickness. He seems to be grief-stricken due to the loss of a friend. Do you know if this elephant had a very close friendship with anyone?'

They told him how the royal elephant and the stray dog

were best friends. 'What happened to this stray dog?' asked the minister. 'He was taken by an unknown man,' they replied, 'and we do not know where he is now.'

The minister returned to the king and said, 'Your majesty, I am happy to say your elephant is not sick. As strange as it may sound, he became best friends with a stray dog! Since the dog has been taken away, the elephant is grief-stricken and does not feel like eating or drinking or bathing. This is my opinion.'

The king said, 'Friendship is one of life's most wonderful things. My minister, how can we bring back my elephant's friend and make him happy again?'

'My lord,' replied the minister, 'I suggest you make an official announcement that whoever has the dog who used to live at the royal elephant shed will be fined.'

This was done, and when the villager heard of it, he released the dog from his house. He was filled with great happiness and ran as fast as he could, straight back to his best friend, the royal bull elephant.

The elephant was so overjoyed, that he picked up his friend with his trunk and sat him on top of his head. The happy dog wagged his tail, while the elephant's eyes sparkled with delight. They both lived happily ever after.

Meanwhile, the king was very pleased by his elephant's full recovery. He was amazed that his minister seemed to be able to read the mind of an elephant. So he rewarded him appropriately.

The moral is: Even 'natural enemies' can become 'best friends.'

The Bull Called Delightful

Once upon a time, in the country of Gandhara in northern India, there was a city called Takkasila. In that city the Enlightenment Being was born as a certain calf. Since he was well bred for strength, he was bought by a high class rich man. He became very fond of the gentle animal, and called him 'Delightful'. He took good care of him and fed him only the best.

When Delightful grew up into a big, fine, strong bull, he thought, 'I was brought up by this generous man. He gave me such good food and constant care, even though sometimes there were difficulties. Now I am a big grown-up bull and there is no other bull who can pull as heavy a load as I can. Therefore, I would like to use my strength to give something in return to my master.'

So he said to the man, 'Sir, please find some wealthy merchant who is proud of having many strong bulls. Challenge him by saying that your bull can pull one hundred heavily loaded bullock carts.'

Following his advice, the high class rich man went to such a merchant and struck up a conversation. After a while, he brought up the idea of who had the strongest bull in the city.

The merchant said, 'Many have bulls, but no one has any as strong as mine.' The rich man said, 'Sir, I have a bull who can pull one hundred heavily loaded bullock carts.' 'No, friend, how can there be such a bull? That is unbelievable!' said the merchant. The other replied, 'I do have such a bull, and I am willing to make a bet.'

The merchant said, 'I will bet a thousand gold coins that your bull cannot pull a hundred loaded bullock carts.' So the bet was made and they agreed on a date and time for the challenge.

The merchant attached together one hundred big bullock carts. He filled them with sand and gravel to make them very heavy.

The high class rich man fed the finest rice to the bull called Delightful. He bathed him and decorated him and hung a beautiful garland of flowers around his neck.

Then he harnessed him to the first cart and climbed up onto it. Being so high class, he could not resist the urge to make himself seem very important. So he cracked a whip in the air, and yelled at the faithful bull, 'Pull, you dumb animal! I command you to pull, you big dummy!'

The bull called Delightful thought, 'This challenge was my idea. I have never done anything bad to my master, and yet he insults me with such hard and harsh words!' So he remained in his place and refused to pull the carts.

The merchant laughed and demanded his winnings from the bet. The high class rich man had to pay him the one thousand gold coins. He returned home and sat down, saddened by his lost bet, and embarrassed by the blow to his pride.

The bull called Delightful grazed peacefully on his way home. When he arrived, he saw his master sadly lying on his side. He asked, 'Sir, why are you lying there like that? Are you sleeping? You look sad.' The man said, 'I lost a thousand gold coins because of you. With such a loss, how could I sleep?'

The bull replied. 'Sir, you called me 'dummy'. You even cracked a whip in the air over my head. In all my life, did I ever break anything, step on anything, make a mess in the wrong place, or behave like a 'dummy' in any way?' He answered, 'No, my pet.'

The bull called Delightful said, 'Then sir, why did you call me 'dumb animal', and insult me even in the presence of others? The fault is yours. I have done nothing wrong. But since I feel sorry for you, go again to the merchant and make the same bet for two thousand gold coins. And remember to use only the respectful words I deserve so well.'

Then the high class rich man went back to the merchant and made the bet for two thousand gold coins. The merchant thought it would be easy money. Again he set up the one hundred heavily loaded bullock carts. Again the rich man fed and bathed the bull, and hung a garland of flowers around his neck.

When all was ready, the rich man touched Delightful's forehead with a lotus blossom, having given up the whip. Thinking of him as fondly as if he were his own child, he said, 'My son, please do me the honour of pulling these one hundred bullock carts.'

Lo and behold, the wonderful bull pulled with all his might and dragged the heavy carts, until the last one stood in the place of the first.

The merchant, with his mouth hanging open in disbelief, had to pay the two thousand gold coins. The onlookers were so impressed that they honoured the bull called Delightful with gifts. But even more important to the high class rich man than his winnings was his valuable lesson in humility and respect.

The moral is: Harsh words bring no reward. Respectful words bring honour to all.

Grandma's Blackie

Once upon a time, when King Brahmadatta was ruling in Benares, there was an old woman who had a calf. This calf was of a noble dark colour. In fact, he was jet black without a spot of white. He was the Bodhisatta—the Enlightened Being.

The old woman raised the little calf just as though he were her own child. She fed him only the very best rice and rice porridge. She petted his head and neck, and he licked her hand. Since they were so friendly, the people began calling the calf, 'Grandma's Blackie'.

Even after he grew up into a big strong bull, Grandma's Blackie remained very tame and gentle. The village children played with him, holding onto his neck and ears and horns. They would even grab his tail and swing up onto his back for a ride. He liked children, so he never complained.

The friendly bull thought, 'The loving old woman, who brought me up, is like a kind mother to me. She raised me as if I were her own child. She is poor and in need, but too humble to ask for my help. She is too gentle to force me to work. Because I also love her, I wish to release her from the suffering of poverty.' So he began looking for work.

One day a caravan of 500 carts came by the village. It stopped at a difficult place to cross the river. The bullocks were not able to pull the carts across. The caravan leader hooked up all 500 pairs of bullocks to the first cart. But the river was so rough that they could not pull across even that one cart.

Faced with this problem, the leader began looking for more bulls. He was known to be an expert judge of the qualities of bulls. While examining the wandering village herd, he noticed Grandma's Blackie. At once he thought, 'This noble bullock looks like he has the strength and the will to pull my carts across the river.'

He said to the villagers standing nearby, 'To whom does this big black bull belong? I would like to use him to pull my caravan across the river, and I am willing to pay his owner for his services.' The people said, 'By all means, take him. His master is not here.'

So he put a rope through Grandma's Blackie's nose. But when he pulled, he could not budge him! The bull was thinking, 'Until this man says what he will pay for my work, I will not move.'

Being such a good judge of bulls, the caravan leader understood his reasoning. So he said, 'My dear bull, after you have pulled my 500 carts across the river, I will pay you two gold coins for each cart—not just one, but two!' Hearing this, Grandma's Blackie went with him at once.

Then the man harnessed the strong black bull to the first cart. He proceeded to pull it across the river. This was what all one thousand bulls could not do before. Likewise, he pulled across each of the other 499 carts, one at a time, without slowing down a bit!

When all was done, the caravan leader made a package containing only one gold coin per cart, that is, 500 coins. He hung this around the mighty bullock's neck. The bull thought, 'This man promised two gold coins per cart, but that is not what he has hung around my neck. So I will not let him leave!' He went to the front of the caravan and blocked the path.

The leader tried to push him out of the way, but he would not move. He tried to drive the carts around him. But all the bulls had seen how strong he was, so they would not move either!

The man thought, 'There is no doubt that this is a very intelligent bull, who knows I have given him only half-pay.' So he made a new package containing the full one thousand gold coins, and hung it instead around the bull's neck.

Then Grandma's Blackie re-crossed the river and walked directly towards the old woman, his 'mother'. Along the way, the children tried to grab the money package, thinking it was a game. But he escaped them.

When the woman saw the heavy package, she was surprised. The children told her all about what happened down at the river. She opened the package and discovered the one thousand gold coins.

The old woman also saw the tired look in the eyes of her 'child'. She said, 'Oh my son, do you think I wish to live off the money you earn? Why did you wish to work so hard and suffer so? No matter how difficult it may be, I will always care for and look after you.'

Then the kind woman washed the lovely bull and massaged his tired muscles with oil. She fed him good food and cared for him, until the end of their happy lives together.

The moral is: Loving-kindness makes the poorest house into the richest home.

Big Red, Little Red and No-squeal

Once upon a time, there were two calves who were part of a country household. At the same home there also lived a girl and a baby pig. Since he hardly ever made a sound, the pig was called 'No-squeal'.

The masters of the house treated No-squeal very, very well. They fed him large amounts of the very best rice, and even rice porridge with rich brown sugar.

The two calves noticed this. They worked hard pulling ploughs in the fields and bullock carts on the roads. Little Red said to Big Red, 'My big brother, in this household you and I do all the hard work. We bring prosperity to the family. But they feed us only grass and hay. The baby pig No-squeal does nothing to support the family. And yet they feed him the finest and fanciest of foods. Why should he get such special treatment?'

The wise elder brother said, 'Oh young one, it is dangerous to envy anybody. Therefore, do not envy the baby pig for being fed such rich food. What he eats is really 'the food of death'.

'There will soon be a marriage ceremony for the daughter of the house, and little No-squeal will be the wedding feast! That's why he is being pampered and fed in such rich fashion.

'In a few days the guests will arrive. Then this piglet will be dragged away by the legs, killed, and made into curry for the feast.'

Sure enough, in a few days the wedding guests arrived. The baby pig No-squeal was dragged away and killed. And just as Big Red had said, he was cooked in various types of curries and devoured by the guests.

Then Big Red said, 'My dear young brother, did you see what happened to baby No-squeal?' 'Yes brother,' replied Little Red, 'now I understand.'

Big Red continued, 'This is the result of being fed such rich food. Our poor grass and hay are a hundred times better than his rich porridge and sweet brown sugar. For our food brings no harm to us, but instead promises long life!'

The moral is: Don't envy the well-off until you know the price they pay.

Harsha's Experiments

The Emperor Harsha was a daring experimenter in everything. When all people wanted to follow the best religion, Buddhism, Saivism or Sun-worship, he combined the best of all the three. Bana begged of him to become a worshipper of Siva alone, Kumarapala implored him to worship only the sun, and Yuan Chawang exhorted him to follow Buddhism exclusively. Sick of these pesterings, the Emperor wanted to stop them. So, one morning, he sent for Bana and said 'I am thinking of following Buddhism exclusively.' 'Oh, no' said Bana, 'Rather than do that, remain as you are. Worship Siva at least now and then'. 'All right,' said Harsha. He then sent for Kumarapala and told him 'I am thinking of following Buddhism exclusively'. 'Oh, no,' said Kumarapala. 'Rather than do that, Your Majesty will do well to continue as at present and worship the sun also now and then'. Harsha sent him away also and called Yuan Chawang and told him. 'I am thinking of worshipping only Siva hereafter, as he is my family deity.' 'Rather than do that, I request Your Majesty to continue as now, worshipping Siva and the sun now and then, and give Buddhism an honoured place in your heart and court,' said Yuan Chawang. Then Harsha called Bana and Kumarapala ard Yuan Chawang together, and said, 'As desired by all of you, I am going to continue as I am, worshipping Buddha, Siva and the sun. I am glad that you, too, have come to the identical conclusions that I came to before. After all, why should there be any conflict between these religions, all of which are of the Aryas? Why should a man's love for his grandmother and mother stand in the way of his love for his wife or daughter?'

Some days later, there was a discussion in court about schemes for making the land prosperous and the people content. Several five-year plans were agreed upon. One was for planting trees, another for digging wells, a third for repairing tanks, a fourth for clearing forests, a fifth for building houses, rest-houses and temples, and a sixth for constructing roads. 'Still another five-year plan is required to make up the sacred seven,' said Bana, 'As it is the seventh, let the Emperor himself suggest it'. 'All right,' said Harsha. 'Every five years I shall empty the state treasury by distributing everything to the poor and then shall receive presents from the rich to replenish the treasury'. 'It is a new idea,' said Bana. 'Perhaps,' Harsha said, 'but I am not ashamed of originality. Nor should we fight shy of new ideas. It the rains can fill our tanks, why should not the rich pour out their treasures to fill the poor men's bellies?' The resolution was adopted owing to the earnest insistence of the king. On three five-yearly festivals, Harsha emptied the treasury and replenished it by taking gifts from the nobles and the rich. But he found that the Buddhist and Brahmin priests knocked off the major portion of the wealth and that the genuine poor got but little. So he abolished the custom and diverted the money to digging wells. 'Better that the rains fill the wells than flow to the ocean,' he said. His five-year plan has never again been revived.

Devotion Tells

One hot morning, Emperor Kanishka was going out for a ride incognito in his dominions. He saw a shepherd boy busy erecting a mud pagoda in a field by the wayside, and smiled to himself. Late in the afternoon, when he was returning, he saw the boy still at it. It had become six feet high with mud walls all round. The emperor was pleased at the boy's devotion. He went to him and asked, 'What are you doing, my boy?' 'I am building a pagoda,' said the boy. 'For whom?' 'For the great Buddha.' 'How small a temple for such a great one!' said Kanishka. The shepherd boy, who had never seen the emperor, replied, 'I am not the Emperor Kanishka that I can construct a big and mighty temple. Each man must build according to his ability and means. There is no shame in doing one's best, sir. I am a poor shepherd boy and can only construct such a structure.' The emperor was struck by the boy's fine devotion and asked him, 'My boy, if the Emperor Kanishka were to construct a temple, how high do you think it should be?' 'Four hundred feet sir,' said the boy,' 'and it should have a gold image of Buddha. But where is the chance of the emperor building any temple, sir? Only we poor folk must do what we can.'

Kanishka went to his palace and gave orders for the construction of a big pagoda four hundred feet high and with a gold image of the Buddha. It took seven years to build. When it was ready, he sent for the shepherd boy who had by then become a monk. The monk came in to see the emperor who was in his imperial robes and could not be recognized as the lonely rider of that hot summer day. 'Brother,' said Kanishka, 'You said once that I would never construct a pagoda. I have built this one. Is it to your liking?' 'Splendid, sire,' said the monk. 'I am sorry I told that horseman some silly things that day. But I said what I felt and never expected him to tell Your Majesty. I beg your pardon sire, but still, I am glad, as the good cause has profited by my indiscretion.' 'I am that horseman,' said Kanishka, taking off his robes and showing himself in the old rider's dress, 'and I make you chief priest of this temple; carry on with the faith of old.'

Wings Not Grown Yet

In the Parana monastery in the Deccan, dedicated to Kasyapa Buddha, the Buddha prior to Gautama Buddha, there were five storeys, all scooped out of the living rock. The first storey had five hundred cells, the second four hundred, the third three hundred, the fourth two hundred and the fifth one hundred. There was a perennial water supply from a spring on the top story which was made to circle round and round supplying every cell. There was no cultivation near by. Nor was there any civilised village close by. Seven miles away there was a Bhil village. The inmates thereof believed that the Buddhist monks could fly to the monastery. One day, they met some Chinese pilgrims walking to the monastery. 'Why do you walk? Why don't you fly.' asked the Bhils 'We are but novices in the religion. Our wings are not grown yet,' was the perfectly convincing reply.

Asoka and his Viceroys

Asoka once called all his viceroys to Pataliputra on the occasion of his birthday and told them that the best of them would be awarded a pair of valuable gold bangles. He then asked them all to state their respective claims. 'Sire,' said the Viceroy or Suvarnagiri, 'I have trebled the quantity of gold sent to the emperor from my province. Never were the revenues so great, or so promptly collected.'

'And I,' said the Viceroy of Tosali, 'I have reduced the expenses by one half and crushed the spirit of the Kalingas, and made the forest Khonds and Savaras fear us.'

'And I,' said the Viceroy of Takshasila, 'I have kept the frontiers safe and made the tribesmen and people feel the might of the Mauryan Raj.'

'And I,' said the Viceroy of Ujjaini. 'I have increased the expenditure two-fold and cut down the revenues paid by the people by one half. Formerly, a great sum was being paid to the imperial exchequer by my predecessors in excess of the fixed contribution. All that goes back now to the province itself in useful and remunerative investments. I have spent a million on the Sudarsana lake in Girnar and made famine impossible there. The rest of the money goes to the upkeep of additional hospitals, rest-house, temples, *viharas* and schools and to the propagation of the knowledge of Dharma.'

'The Viceroy of Ujjaini gets the prize!' said Asoka. 'Mere

sending of gold is not the duty of a viceroy; nor is decrease of expenditure or increase of revenue or defence of the frontier or instilling fear of our Raj or crushing the spirit of a people. A viceroy represents me and I expect him to do his duty by the people entrusted to his charge. The real gold he can send to me is in the shape of more tanks and wells, more trees, more schools, more rest-houses, more temples, more *viharas,* more hospitals, more enlightenment among the people entrusted to his charge and greater dissemination of the knowledge of Dharma among them.'

The Perfect Wife

A man in Ancient India went in search of a perfect wife. After an arduous search, he found such a lady who consented to be his wife. They were married, and the husband was joyous, beyond all measure, at his having secured such a wife. One day, he told his friend that he was the most fortunate man on earth, that he had a wife who in beauty, virtue and all other good qualities, excelled all other women on earth, and that he was very proud of this fact. He went home and told his wife about this conversation. 'My dear,' said she, 'pride is a demon, you should avoid it at all costs.' The husband felt a little chilled, but kept silent.

Some days later, a naughty child threw a stone which hit the husband on the forehead, causing blood to flow freely. The infuriated husband rushed after the urchin with a stick swearing to give it a jolly good thrasing. His wife caught hold of him and said, 'My dear, you should not get so angry. Anger is one of the worst enemies of man. The child, in its ignorance, threw the stone at you: it is not for you to imitate it in its childishness.' The husband felt this advice to be ideal, but lacking in sympathy. Another day, the husband bought a basket of excellent mangoes and expressed his intention of eating a dozen of them at one sitting. 'My dear,' admonished his wife, 'that would be gluttony, and no one should be gluttonous. Eat one or two fruits and be satisfied.' A doubt crossed the poor husband's mind whether he had, after all, been wise in marrying this perfect wife. Some days later, the husband got five rupees for doing hard work, for which he had expected to be paid at least fifteen rupees. He was dissatisfied, and expressed his dissatisfaction in no uncertain terms. 'My dear,' remonstrated his wife, 'you should never be dissatisfied. Contentment is the secret of happiness. Be contented with whatever you get.' The husband bit his lips and remained silent. He was fast repenting his folly in having married this perfect woman. The next day, his house was burnt down, and he was grieving over it. 'My dear,' advised his wife, 'do not give way to futile grief. A wise man should neither grieve nor rejoice.' This was the limit. He rushed to his friend, told him everything, and wailed 'What a blockhead I was in having married this perfect woman!' 'Do you know what Buddha said to Ananda about women just before he passed away?' asked the friend. 'No. Tell me'. 'Ananda asked Buddha 'Oh Exalted One, how should one behave towards women?' 'By not seeing them, Ananda.' 'Suppose we see them?' 'Don't talk to them, Ananda'. 'Suppose they talk to us?' 'Keep wide awake, Ananda, and don't be surprised if your peace of mind is gone for ever.' No wonder your peace of mind is gone' said the friend. 'Ah, Buddha was certainly the wisest among men,' said the husband. 'I must seek refuge in him,' and went and forthwith entered a Buddhist monastery and became a monk, forgetting his perfect wife without the least regret.